*Introduction to*  Bookbinding

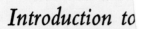

*by the same author*
BOOKBINDING THEN AND NOW (1959)

# INTRODUCTION
## TO
# BOOK
# BINDING

## by

## Lionel S. Darley

*with sketches by*
*the author*

## Faber and Faber

First published in 1965
First published in Faber Paperbacks 1976
by Faber and Faber Limited
3 Queen Square London WC1
Printed in Great Britain by
Redwood Burn Limited, Trowbridge & Esher
All rights reserved

ISBN 0 571 11082 7 (Faber Paperbacks)
ISBN 0 571 11105 X (hard-bound edition)

# Contents

# RE-BINDING OLD BOOKS

## BINDING IN LEATHER

## MACHINE BOOKBINDING

# *Plates*

# Author's Note

Prices appearing in the following pages belong to 1965, the year of original publication, and are no longer relevant. Present day costs of the items concerned may be obtained from the following suppliers:

PAPER of all kinds          T. N. Lawrence & Son Ltd
2 Bleeding Heart Yard
London EC1

TOOLS and equipment     Dryad Handicrafts
Northgates
Leicester

TYPE and hand letters      T. Mackrell & Co Ltd.,
Industrial Estate
Colchester Road
Witham, Essex

L.S.D.
1977

# Introduction to Bookbinding

Bookbinding as a spare-time occupation is a hobby that gives supreme satisfaction to anyone who enjoys making things with his own hands and who feels the need of some artistic activity. It is an ancient craft with its origins far back in history, when gospels and psalters for use in religious services were inscribed on vellum and bound in leather in the monasteries. The binding methods and, indeed, many of the tools employed in making those early books have come down through the centuries almost unchanged, and are still used today by the master craftsman and by the student working in craft schools. So the amateur in striving to perfect himself in the 'Art, Mystery and Manual Occupation', as the Elizabethan Statue of Apprentices described bookbinding, will feel his pleasure in a beautiful craft enhanced by the knowledge that every operation is based on age-old tradition.

Handbinding is not an easy craft to learn; there are no short cuts to achievement; it demands from its followers, patience, great neatness in working, as much good taste as can be diligently cultivated and a steadfast determination to succeed. The progress of the student is often beset with difficulties, especially in the early stages, but each obstacle mastered is a lesson learned and success when it comes is infinitely rewarding. Cobden-Sanderson who became one of the most famous English binders, was familiar with the disappointments of the beginner. In his diary he records his early failures in tooling the cover of *In Memoriam*. He wrote, 'I could spit upon the book, throw it out of the window, into the fire, upon the ground and grind it with my heel.' Yet a year and a half later, when at last he succeeded in completing the tooling of the cover, it was considered one of his most perfect bindings.

Books are among the treasured possessions of most people so there is a special satisfaction in the ability to keep them in good condition, to understand their construction so as to make workman-like repairs when needed, or to re-cover in new bindings of one's own devising any which have become dilapidated through hard use or age; or again, to be able to take a few sheets of writing-paper, fold them to a convenient size, sew them and mould them into conventional book form, make a neat cover from strawboard, covered with cloth or patterned paper, and then by uniting book and cover, to produce a notebook or diary for one's own use. These are not only rewarding occupations in themselves but also, with care and application, they can become exercises by which the student gradually builds up that knowledge of the binding craft and the manual dexterity in the use of the tools of the trade, the folding-stick, the needle and thread, the plough, glue brush, paster and backing hammer, which in time will bring within his capabilities the achievement which must be the ambition of every student of hand binding, the book worthily bound in full leather in the traditional manner, with raised bands, and the cover lettered and tooled in gleaming gold.

## The Binder's Tools

The tools the hand binder requires are few and simple, and the beginner is well advised to start with bare necessities and add to his equipment as the need arises. Among the first essentials are a bone folding-stick (which has many uses besides folding), a packet of bookbinder's needles, a pair of 6" scissors, a cobbler's knife, a pint-size glue pot, a round 1" glue brush, a paste pot (a lb. size earthenware honey jar is

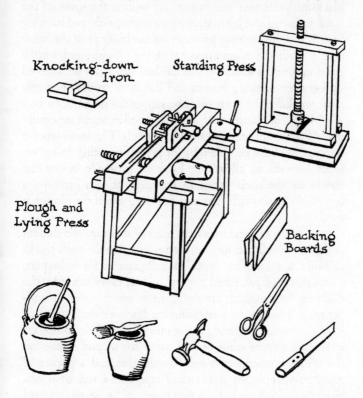

Knocking-down
Iron

Standing Press

Plough and
Lying Press

Backing
Boards

just right for this) and a 1½" flat paint brush to use with it; an old litho stone about 10" by 15" in size or a similar slab of smooth flat marble or stone on which to knock up books, pare leather and do the many jobs that require a firm, even surface to work on.

The largest item in the list of essential equipment for the

amateur binder is the lying press, costing about £5. This press is made of beechwood blocks, operated by wooden screws, and should have one side grooved to take the cutting plough. The lying press is to a binder what the anvil is to a blacksmith; its uses are numerous; with it the spine of the book is shaped and jointed, using two wedge-shaped backing boards and the backing hammer; in the lying press the book is held while the edges are cut with the plough; and, until a standing press is installed, the finished book can be screwed up between pressing boards and left there to dry. For efficient working the press must be supported on an open box 2' 6" high, or, better still, on the wooden stand especially made for the purpose and known as a tub. This stand sets the lying press at the right height for proper working and gives space beneath to allow the book to protrude below the cheeks of the press when so required; it also provides a receptacle into which shavings can drop when the plough is used.

In addition to these necessary tools of the trade the student will find it useful, as he goes along, to assemble small stocks of paper, a quire of 20" × 30" cartridge paper for endpapers, a few sheets of patterned papers, such as those made by the Curwen Press, which are excellent as cover paper or endpaper; a yard or two of Sundour book-cloth; a yard of muslin or mull for lining the spines of cloth-bound books; a sheet or two of stout brown paper for second linings on the spine; a pound of good flexible glue and a packet of paste powder; some unbleached tape and a reel of bookbinder's linen thread 16s; a few sheets of 24 oz. strawboard for cloth work and some millboard for leather-bound books. Boards and paper should be kept flat, preferably packed together with a plywood stiffener to prevent warping.

## A Room to Work In

At this point it will have become evident to the beginner who intends to work at home that one of the first considerations is where he can conveniently keep this equipment. There are obvious difficulties in stowing it away in a cupboard, however commodious, to be brought out only when wanted for use; the lying press and its stand are too cumbersome for easy movement; and in bookbinding there are many occasions when partly completed work should be left to dry, safe from disturbance. The ideal solution is, of course, to have a small room, or perhaps a shed in the garden if it can be suitably warmed, which can be set aside and used only for bookbinding, some little place that can be fitted out as a workshop and made comfortable, with a solid table or bench before a window giving good light, and a movable lamp overhead so that work can proceed at any convenient time.

On the table should be a flat electric boiling ring on which to heat the glue pot or hand tools when required, as well as to add to the warmth of the room. The proper warming up of the work room is an essential since neither glue nor gold tooling can be worked in a chill atmosphere. On the table also, a place must be found for the flat paring stone, with knives, scissors, folding-sticks, etc. all set out conveniently handy. The lying press on its stand must also be placed within easy reach of the light; with a little ingenuity this may be covered with a movable wooden lid, thus providing another work bench at just the right height for the many jobs that have to be done standing. Finally a shelf or two, and a roomy cupboard or chest of drawers will provide necessary storage space for everything not required for immediate use, so that table and work bench are always cleared for action. Inevitably there are times when the place tends to get in a muddle, but the desirability of being neat and tidy must always be kept in mind; it facilitates work and reduces to a minimum the danger of outside assistance in such matters, which may well frustrate the best-laid plans.

## How to Make a Start

But of course, before any of these preparations to become a bookbinder, indeed before buying anything beyond the simplest tools, the student will be well advised to seek some practical experience in the subject by attending classes at a technical school. In all craft work it is essential to start on the right lines and to learn from the expert how to do the various operations in the way experience has proved best. When Robinson Crusoe on his desert island needed a plank he chopped down a tree and adzed away its rotundity until he got a flat length of wood. The student of bookbinding left to his own devices may well fall into methods similarly wasteful of time and material. It is here that the guidance of a good teacher and the inspiration and encouragement to be gained from working among others battling with the same problems, is so valuable to the beginner. In a craft school the student becomes familiar with the names of tools and processes, discovers when not to use glue if paste will do, and learns easily and naturally a hundred and one do's and don'ts, and other small scraps of information that are hard to come by if alone with an instruction book.

However, if bookbinding is to reveal all its delights as a spare time occupation, a recreation that is to lead to satisfying achievement, the craft school is only the beginning. The real development of the student's capabilities will come when he puts their teaching to the proof by working unaided in the privacy of his own little work room, using his own tools and materials and the knowledge they have given him, to bind a book of his own choosing in a cover designed and fashioned to reveal whatever skill and art the gods may have blessed him with.

## Binding Processes

The processes of hand binding are traditionally divided into two departments known as 'forwarding' and 'finishing'. The forwarder binds the book, the finisher decorates the spine and sides of the cover. Forwarding therefore consists of all the stages of binding from folding to covering, though it may be noted in passing that in modern factory usage the term forwarding is applied only to men's work which starts with the sewn book; the earlier operations from folding to sewing being known as 'the women's departments'. In the

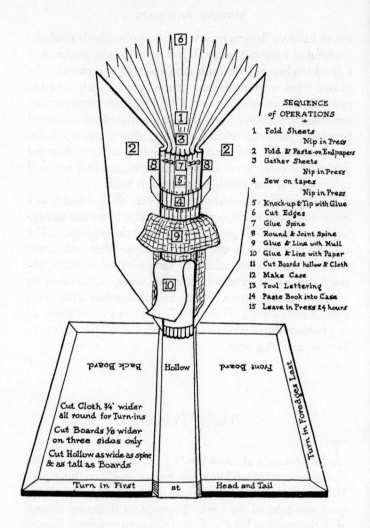

SEQUENCE
of OPERATIONS

1  Fold Sheets
        Nip in Press
2  Fold & Paste-on Endpapers
3  Gather Sheets
        Nip in Press
4  Sew on tapes
        Nip in Press
5  Knock-up & Tip with Glue
6  Cut Edges
7  Glue Spine
8  Round & Joint Spine
9  Glue & Line with Mull
10 Glue & Line with Paper
11 Cut Boards hollow & Cloth
12 Make Case
13 Tool Lettering
14 Paste Book into Case
15 Leave in Press 24 hours

Back Board     Hollow     Front Board

Cut Cloth ¾" wider
all round for Turn-ins

Cut Boards ⅛ wider
on three sides only

Cut Hollow as wide as spine
& as tall as Boards

Turn in Foredges Last

Turn in First     at     Head and Tail

16

older sense however forwarding included all the following:

(1) Folding flat sheets into sections.
(2) Inserting plates, etc. end/papering.
(3) Collating.
(4) Sewing on tapes or cords.
(5) Cutting the edges.
(6) Knocking-up square and gluing spine.
(7) Rounding the spine.
(8) Backing or jointing the spine.
(9) Gluing and lining with mull.
(10) Gluing and lining with brown paper.
(11) Cutting boards, hollow and cloth.
(12) Making a case or covering.
(13) Lettering and decorating the cover.
(14) Pasting the book into the case.
(15) Putting the book in the press and leaving to dry.

When binding a book in leather in the orthodox manner the edges may be cut 'in boards'. This will entail a change in the above order of procedure since the edges have to be cut after the spine has been rounded and backed, and the boards laced to the sewing cords. Then items 9 and 10 will be omitted, and, instead, the backed spine will have the glue cleaned off with paste and then left to dry. This softening the glue with paste and cleaning off renders the spine hard and springy so that it returns to its rounded shape after being knocked flat for the fore-edge cut.

# Making a Notebook

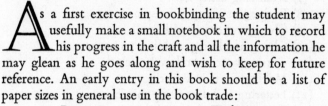

As a first exercise in bookbinding the student may usefully make a small notebook in which to record his progress in the craft and all the information he may glean as he goes along and wish to keep for future reference. An early entry in this book should be a list of paper sizes in general use in the book trade:

| Paper size | | Book size |
| --- | --- | --- |
| ROYAL | 25″ × 20″ | 10″ × 6¼″ |
| MEDIUM | 23″ × 18″ | 9″ × 5¾″ |
| DEMY | 22½″ × 17½″ | 8¼″ × 5⅝″ |
| CROWN | 20″ × 15″ | 7½″ × 5″ |

The paper required for a NOTEBOOK should be writing-paper which will differ in size from book paper. A quire of 16½″ × 21″ costing about 5s. will make two handy little books of 160 pages each, 8¼″ tall by 5⅛″ wide, when the edges are cut. By following such a book through all the stages of its development from a pile of flat paper into two neat books, the student will be able to get a working knowledge of the processes of bookbinding.

## Folding

Folding is the first operation in binding a book. The fold unites two leaves of paper, thus forming a 4 page, the basic element from which all books are made; into the centre of that fold go the sewing stitches which unite all the four pages of which the book is in fact composed; on to the back of that fold goes the glue which enables the spine to be moulded by rounding and backing, to form the conventional convex book shape: on to it, also, are finally glued the linings of mull and brown paper which hold all strongly together. The fold therefore is of prime importance in the book's construction: it must be made square and sharp.

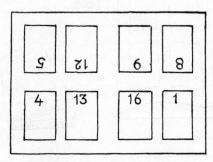

16 page sheet - 8 backed by 8

Although the amateur is rarely required to fold printed sheets—any unbound book he is able to buy will probably be supplied by the publisher ready folded for convenience in packing—he should, nevertheless, acquire the habit of folding even plain paper in the accepted way. Books are normally printed sixteen pages on a sheet—eight pages backed by eight pages—the pages being arranged in a way to suit one of the various folding machines, the simplest arrangement being that in which three right-angle folds bring the pages into numerical order. At the foot of page 1 of each sheet a signature mark is printed, either a letter or a number, to indicate the beginning of a section. To fold this type of sheet correctly the student places it with this signature mark face down on the table, so that page 2 is under his left hand

and page 3 is away on the extreme right of the sheet. He then brings that right-hand side of the sheet over the left, so that page 3 faces down on page 2, and the print of the opposing pages is in exact register: he then makes the fold by passing the folding-stick firmly and evenly from bottom to top of the folded edge up the paper. Next the upper

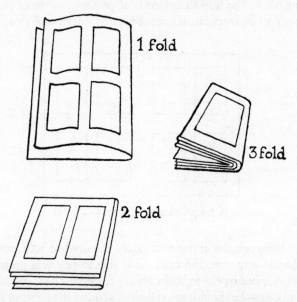

pages of the now doubled paper are brought down precisely over the lower pages and the fold made along the top edge. Finally the right side of the sheet, now eight pages thick, is brought over to register above the left and folded. Before making each fold care must be taken to ensure that the print of opposing pages registers exactly, and are firmly held there with the left hand while the right hand makes the fold. When folding paper that is already doubled or doubled again, as in the second and third fold, it is necessary to hold the folding-stick firmly across the sheet near its centre, while the left hand, pulling against the stick, brings the upper half of the paper over it and down into position. This ensures the inner and outer pages folding tight up to each other. After making the second fold it is useful to slit half-way along the heads; this prevents creases forming in the gutter when the last fold is made.

All this may make folding appear a rather complicated business, and, of course, doing it well is not at first easy. It may be some comfort to the beginner to reflect that women hand-folders in the trade turn out two or three hundred sheets an hour; ease comes with practice. Such work, however, is now mostly done by machines folding some two thousand sheets an hour, which happens to be the same output as was claimed for the first folding-machine invented in 1850 by William Black. The greatly increased production of modern folding-machines is obtained by folding paper four times the size of William Black's, on which are printed four sixteen-page sections, arranged so as to fold simultaneously, thus producing eight thousand sections an hour.

The first thing we have to do, then, in making our notebook is to fold the quire of writing-paper into sixteen-page sections, following the method described above—first fold, from right to left, halves the length of paper, second fold from top to bottom halves the width, and the final fold from right to left again, so a sheet of paper becomes one section of sixteen pages.

When all the sheets are folded in this way, a pair of four-page endpapers should be cut, folded and stuck to the first and last sections of the book by an edging of paste $\frac{1}{8}''$ wide. In cutting the endpapers care must be taken to see the grain of the paper runs from head to tail; the direction of the grain can usually be found by folding an offcut, first one way, then the other; the fold that goes smoothly and easily is the way of the grain. If it is desired to have a coloured or patterned paper for the ends, it is well to choose the cover material at the same time, to make certain both harmonize. Having allowed the paste time to set, the sheets should be stacked in a neat pile, reversing half the sheets so as to avoid all the folds being on the same sides; put a strawboard of about the right size at each end, knock-up square, and then, holding the pile tight, proceed to hammer evenly around the edges to consolidate the folds. A short time in the press will help to this end and prevent loose sewing.

## Sewing

Before starting to sew it is necessary to work out the proper positions for the tapes and stitches along the spine; the first and last stitches, known as the kettle-stitches, should be placed about $\frac{1}{2}''$ from the top and rather more, say $\frac{5}{8}''$, from the tail of the book: the first tape should go about

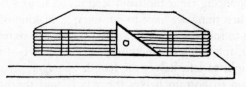

Marking-up for Sewing Three Tapes

1" below the top kettle-stitch, and the second tape about $1\frac{1}{4}''$ above the lower kettle-stitch. These points are pencilled on the spine fold of the first section, six marks in all; the sewing-needle will go in at the top kettle-stitch mark, come out above and re-enter below the first tape, out and in again round the second tape to finally emerge at the lower kettle-stitch mark. Using this marked sheet as a guide, now punch a small neat hole with a bodkin or cobbler's awl in the dead centre of the spine fold of each sheet, from the inside outwards, to show where each stitch is to go and so ensure a workman-like alignment of the sewing down the spine of the book.

Sewing on Tapes

When all the sheets are neatly holed, cut two pieces of tape about three times the width of the spine, bend them 'L' shape and fix with cellotape to a board in their required positions. Now lay the first sheet, page one, down on the board, spine against the upturned tapes and towards the worker, place the left hand inside the centre of the sheet, and, with the right hand, push the needle through the top kettle-stitch hole, where the left hand takes it and immediately carries it down to emerge above the first tape. And

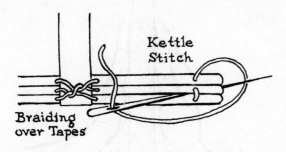

Kettle Stitch

Braiding over Tapes

so on down the length of the sheet, in and out, and round the outside of each tape, the needle finally emerging through the lower kettle-stitch hole. Repeat the motions up the length of the second sheet, starting at the lower kettle-stitch hole and passing the needle under the thread where it crosses each tape on the first sheet. On emerging at the top again pull tight the thread in both sheets, and knot. Continue the process in each of remaining sheets, looping the thread over each tape, and when the sewing of each sheet is completed, pull the thread tight, pass the needle round the kettle-stitch in the previous sheet and through the loop of thread thus formed, to make a tied chain of sewing across the

Weaver's knot

top and tail of the spine. In sewing it is important that the thread should be equally tight in all sections, irregular tension in the stitches may cause some inner leaves to work

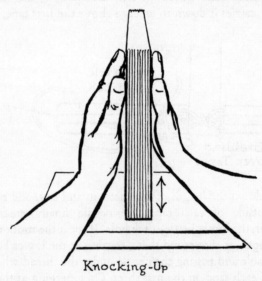

Knocking-Up

loose, and make good, even rounding and backing more difficult later on. When one length of thread is nearly used up, another piece is tied to it by a weaver's knot which makes a small flat join. A slip-knot is made in the new thread and the old thread passed through it. The long end of the new thread is then pulled down, drawing with it a loop of the old thread through the slip-knot. This knot should be made as close as possible to the book, leaving only enough old thread to bring the knot inside the section.

The book should now be knocked-up square at head and spine and hammered along the back edge to reduce the swelling caused by the sewing. Then the spine should be tipped in two places (not all along) with thin hot glue, knocked-up square again and left to set under a weight. Finally an extra leaf of paper should be placed at front and back and kept in position by two tiny spots of paste on the spine edge, to act as a protection leaf over the endpapers.

## Cutting the Edges

This notebook being a first exercise in binding and the student possibly working in a class where a guillotine is available, a description of the more laborious business of cutting the edges with a plough can be left to a later chapter (see page 70). If this is so it is now only necessary to mark on the front protection leaf where the cuts are to be made at head, tail, and fore-edge, and then leave the actual cutting to someone experienced in the use of guillotines. A good binder will always cut as little as possible off the edges of a book. To clear the bolts (folds) in the head it is usually necessary to cut $\frac{1}{8}''$ from the top edge. The cutting line on the other two edges is decided by measuring the narrowest page in the fore-edge and the shortest in the tail, marking these measurements on the front waste leaf. The cutting line can then be drawn in pencil $\frac{1}{8}''$ inside those marks. The book, having been knocked-up and tipped with glue after it was sewn, will retain its squareness without trouble during the marking and cutting operations.

## Rounding and Backing

The spine must now be glued all along with thin hot glue, care being taken to rub it well in so that it gets down between the sections: the book is again knocked-up at head and fore-edge lest any disturbance has occurred, and left to

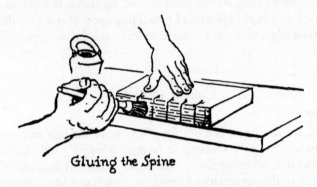

Gluing the Spine

set. When the glue on the spine is no longer tacky to the touch yet not really dry—say within an hour of gluing—the book is ready to be rounded and backed. This process gives the inward curving fore-edge and outward curving spine, which experience has shown to be the shape most useful and proper for a book in order that the pages may be turned easily and its appearance retained after many readings. After folding and sewing, gluing becomes the third unifying operation in binding; it combines and solidifies all the separate sections and the elasticity of the glue transforms the spine into a mouldable whole.

Rounding is achieved by drawing forward the outer sec-

tions, first on one side and then on the other, and aiding and
confirming this shaping movement by hammering all along
both sides of the spine. To do this lay the book on its side on
the paring stone, fore-edge towards the worker, and with
fingers of the left hand spread flat on the endpaper pulling,
thumb against the fore-edge pushing, draw the upper part of
the book forward. This will cause the spine to lift a little and
begin to curve. Then, with the backing hammer in the right
hand, gently tap the upper part of the spine from top to tail,
so that the leaves on that side are forced forward evenly.

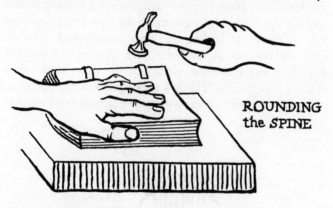

ROUNDING
the SPINE

Now turn the book over and repeat the process on the other
side. The beginner may well find it necessary to go over
both sides more than once before a uniform rounding,
neither too much curve nor too little, is achieved. It is here
that the importance of uniform sewing becomes apparent:
too loose stitches and the leaves slide forward too far; too
tight and rounding becomes difficult.

The book is now ready for backing or jointing, the operation that forms the shoulders on each side of the spine,
against which the board will hinge. The size of the shoulders
is governed by the thickness of boards; for leather binding
the shoulders should be as deep as the boards are thick, but

in cloth-covered books a more pleasing appearance is obtained when the shoulders are a trifle deeper than the board thickness, so that they protrude slightly above the cover level.

Our notebook, which is to have a cloth case, will therefore require shoulders a little deeper than the thickness of the board, say $\frac{3}{32}''$, if a 20-oz. board is used. A pencil line $\frac{3}{32}''$ from the spine must be drawn on the waste sheet on both sides of the book and as the spine has been rounded, the best way to gauge the exact position will be by measuring from the fore-edge. Now take the wedge-shaped backing boards and lay the sharp edge tight up to the pencil line on either side of the book, leaving the tapes outside, and lower all into the lying press until the thick part of the backing boards is just above the surface of the press block: then screw up very tight. This is a tricky job and must be done with care: even the expert will make more than one attempt

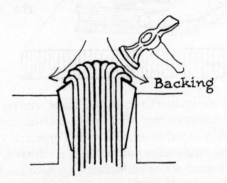

Backing

before he is satisfied he has got the book straight in the press with both backing boards square up to the pencil lines. To prevent the boards slipping about, their inner surfaces should be moistened by a touch of the tongue or a damp rag.

When the book is thus satisfactorily placed and screwed tight in the press, the shoulders are formed by hammering over both sides of the spine, using the backing hammer with an outward sliding motion directed away from the middle of the book, as though it were a block of soft metal on which you wished to form a flange by burring over the edge. The blows of the hammer must be glancing strokes that, without damage to the back, will cause the outer sections—the centre sections should not be hammered—to ride evenly outward and down over the sharp angle of the backing boards so that a uniform lip, projecting at right angles to the sides of the book, is formed along both edges of the spine; it is important that this lip should be hammered firmly on to the downward shape of the backing boards so that when the book is removed from the press, the shoulders are sufficiently bent down for the inevitable slight spring back to leave them in the correct right-angle position. It is worth while taking some trouble in this shaping operation for a well-formed spine, evenly rounded and with equal shoulders on both sides is all important to the good appearance of the finished book.

## Lining the Spine

When the rounding and backing has shaped the spine in a satisfactory manner, it is ready to be lined up with bookbinder's mull and strong brown paper. The mull is cut 2" wider and ½" shorter than the spine of the book; the brown paper should be the full width but ¼" less tall than the spine. Before affixing the linings it is good practice to clean off the old glue from the spine as is done when binding in leather. The way to do this is to give the spine a thin coat of paste, while the book is still in the lying press, leave it to soak for five minutes or so, and then clean it all off, first by scraping off the paste with the folding-stick and then finishing the job with paper shavings or a damp rag. This works the softened glue down between the sections, so repairing any breaks in the gluing that may have resulted from backing, and when thoroughly dry again, leaves the spine hard and springy.

The spine is then given an even coat of glue, moving the brush from the centre upwards and downwards to avoid any overspill on to the edges, the mull is laid in position with equal overlaps on either side and carefully rubbed down with the folding-stick. When this has had time to set, glue the spine a second time, lay the brown paper over the mull, and rub down with a damp rag and the folding-stick, and then put the book between boards laid close up to the joints with the mull inside, and leave to dry under a weight.

The Oxford Hollow

Another way of lining the spine, after the mull has been glued in place, is by making a tubular hollow—sometimes called an Oxford hollow—a device which provides a lining for the spine, a hollow for the cover and an additional point of union between the book and its case. To make this tube a piece of strong brown paper is required, three times as wide and an inch or two longer than the spine of the book. A flap is folded along the length of this paper the precise width of the spine; then the spine of the book is well glued and this folded edge of the paper laid tight up to one side of the spine with an overlap at head and tail. After this has been well rubbed down to ensure the under side sticking firmly all over, the other part of the paper is brought over and is folded tight to the opposite spine edges: thus the paper now has its middle length glued to the book and a loose flap either side. To turn these loose flaps into a tube, the flap that is the same width as the spine is brought over, glued on its outside and then covered by the second wider fold, taking care to draw both close and tight to the spine of the book, and smoothing them down neatly. This type of Oxford hollow is known as 'one on and two off'—one layer of paper being attached to the book, while the outer two layers form the hollow of the case. When this tube is quite dry any surplus paper on the centre flap can be folded over and slit away with a sharp knife: the overlap at head and tail is also snipped off flush with the scissors. The book is now ready for its case and is left under a weight to dry.

## Making the Case

The beginner attending classes in a craft school will discover that there is more than one way of making a case for a cloth-bound book. In general the schools favour the method of attaching the boards to the mull lining of the spine and then covering the book in much the same way as when binding in leather when the boards are laced to the sewing-cords in the traditional manner. That is to say the case is made on the book exactly as was done when cloth first came to be used as a covering for books in the eighteen-twenties: not until seven years later, in 1832, did bookbinders reluctantly abandon their old-fashioned ways and make a separate case that would slide under the platen of the Arming press and so enable them to block the spine with a gold lettering.

Attaching the boards to the book adds something to the strength of the binding, especially when the mull is glued between split boards and a tubular hollow is used on the spine of the book: this is well suited for dictionaries and reference books. For books not subject to heavy use a simpler method is to make the case on the bench, separate from the book, and then paste the book into the case, in the normal way of the binding trade, when both are finished and dry.

Whichever method is employed the first thing to do is to cut the boards to size, and select and cut the covering material. For our notebook the boards can be of 24-oz. thickness, and should be cut the size of the book plus an overlap known as 'the square' on the three outer edges. The extent of this overlap or square can best be judged by taking a piece of board rather larger than the book requires, laying it tight against the joint, marking on it in pencil first the book size with a line along head, fore-edge and tail, and then a second line drawn about $\frac{3}{32}''$ outside the first, to show where the cut is to be made to give the desired square. The width of square is a matter of taste, big and thick books look better with a wide square, thin or pocket books need less; on some books a very fine square, known as a pin-head square, can be very attractive.

Cutting the boards is best done on a board chopper if one is available, otherwise it is a job for the plough and press, for it is difficult to cut a 24-oz. board with knife and straight-edge. Before actually cutting the boards it is necessary to make quite sure the lines drawn are square, clearly marked, and fit both sides of the book.

Having cut the boards we must next cut the hollow or stiffener for the spine of the case. This should be of stiff brown paper and cut to the full width of the spine of the book, and the same height as the boards.

Cutting the cloth for the cover and the positioning of the boards when making the case will be much simplified if the student provides himself with a strip of waste board roughly the height of the boards and a full ¼" wider than the hollow, with top and sides cut square, which can then be used as a gauge for the space between the boards wherein the hollow is to be laid. With this gauge and the two boards, all laid square at top, placed in position on the cloth a cutting line can be drawn a full ½" outside all round to provide turn-ins for the cover.

## The Separate Case

Thin glue is required for making the case, spread evenly with brush strokes worked from the middle outward, to avoid getting glue under the edges. When the cloth has been well glued, it is folded over, glue to glue, and left a minute or two to soak. Meanwhile the boards, hollow, and the gauge, the scissors and folding-stick, can all be laid out within easy reach and a newspaper spread on the table, its back edge towards the worker, so that a dirty page will fall down out of the way when a clean one is needed.

In addition to this provision of clean newspaper to work on, the need for clean fingers must not be forgotten. When working with glue the beginner soon discovers how easy it is to get sticky fingers; this nuisance can be reduced to a minimum by cultivating the habit of only touching glued surfaces with one finger and always having a damp cloth handy to wipe it on. Another useful accessory is a bibbed apron on which that finger can be dried, and of course the hands given an occasional polish just to make sure. Nothing is more exasperating than to find a well-made case spoilt by glue spots. And, of course, when glue is used it is a funda-mental to have the room comfortably warm.

Now open out the glued cloth (taking care not to distort it) on the newspaper, and put down the left-hand board in position leaving ½″ of cloth showing on three sides, lay the gauge up to this board and in line with it at the top; put down the second board in like manner; lift out the gauge and insert in its place the hollow with even margins on either side and level with the boards at head and tail. Turn the cloth over to make sure there are no wrinkles and, if there

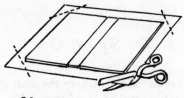

Mitring corners for cloth case

are, smooth them out with the palm of the hand, then reverse the cover again on a clean sheet of the newspaper, square off all the corners with a snip of the scissors ⅛″ away from the board. When each corner has been snipped off in this way the turning in of the overlaps is done first at the head, then the tail and finally on both fore-edges. These turn-ins must be drawn over tight to the board edges and rubbed down neatly all along. When turning in the fore-edge it will be noticed that the cloth of the head and tail margins protrudes slightly beyond the corners of the boards; these protrusions must be bent round with the thumbnail to form a tidy tuck inside the fore-edge cloth margins when those are drawn over and smoothed down with the folding-stick. All these details must be carried out expeditiously so that the case is made and given a final smooth down over all before the glue is quite set. The case can then be stood up and left to dry.

## Case made with Split Boards

Before going on to complete the binding by pasting the book into its case it will be appropriate to consider briefly the alternative ways of making a cloth case for the book. The most important of these is the case made with split boards. This method is intended to give the book sewn on tapes something like the strength of a leather binding, in which the boards have been laced on by the sewing-cords. The boards for this type of cover consist of two thicknesses, a thick board, say 20-oz. outside, and a thin 8-oz. inside, which are glued together and have the mull and tapes of the book held between them. The method of making and attaching split boards is as follows:

Cut a pair of 20-oz. and a pair of 8-oz. boards rather larger than the book requires, glue each pair together, one thick with one thin, leaving an unglued space about $1\frac{1}{2}''$ wide along one side of each. Knock them up square on this unglued edge and at the head, and put in the press to dry.

Meanwhile the book must be prepared to receive the boards; first cut the tapes about $\frac{3}{4}''$ wide and paste them down to the waste sheet that covers the endpaper. Next fold back the mull, glue carefully over the tapes and waste sheet and smooth the mull on to it, creasing the mull tight into the joint with the folding-stick; then fold over the glued waste sheet so that its fore-edge lies along the gutter below the joint and smooth all down neat and close. Turn the book over and repeat the operation on the other side: then lay the book between pressing boards and leave it to dry under a weight. When quite dry the flaps thus formed should be cut down to $1''$ wide.

The boards can now be marked for cutting down to the

correct size which is done by laying them with their unglued edges tight up to the joint of the book and marking them in pencil with the line of the head, tail, and fore-edge, then drawing a second line $\frac{1}{8}''$ outside the first to allow for the squares. The boards can then be cut on a board chopper, or with the lying press and plough.

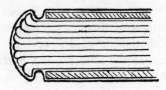

French Joints

With this split-board type of cover it is common practice to bind with French grooves, that is to say, with a space between the joints of the spine and the boards a full $\frac{1}{4}''$ wide, so that when the book comes to be pasted down the cloth at the joint can be forced down into this space to form a deep gully on either side of the spine. This will involve two small changes in case-making procedure: the boards must be cut narrower on the fore-edge by cutting along the book fore-edge line without adding anything for the square: also when gluing the mull and tapes flap into the split, the boards are not laid tight to the joint but, instead, drawn forward an $\frac{1}{8}''$, thus providing the necessary overlap for the fore-edge square.

Whether French grooves are to be used or not, when the boards have been cut to the correct size the unglued portion is opened by bending back the thin board, so that the inner surfaces of both boards of the split may be well glued, after which the flap containing tapes and mull is slipped between and the split closed, first seeing that the thick boards are on the outside. When both front and back boards have been affixed in this way, they must be carefully positioned to give

36

the proper squares all round and the book then placed between pressing boards and left in the press to dry. To avoid any danger of the creased inner board marking the end-

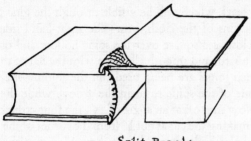

Split Boards

papers it is advisable to lay a tin or thin card between book and boards before screwing up in the press. If the spine has been lined with an Oxford hollow, the making of which is described on page 30, the book and boards are now ready for covering.

## Cutting Cloth for Split-Board Work

The cloth for the cover must now be chosen and cut to size. To find the size required, the book with its boards attached is laid on the reverse side of the cloth and a pencil line drawn round head, fore-edge, and tail, plus a little mark to show where the spine begins: then the book is rolled over (taking care not to let it slip about), a second spine mark and again a line on all the outer boards' edges. The cutting line is now drawn a full ¾″ outside the book-size lines to allow for turn-ins and the cuts made with a sharp knife. Now lay a newspaper on the table, fold towards the worker so that a glued sheet can be easily turned down out of the way, as described earlier: spread and glue the cloth, fold it glue to glue and leave to soak a minute. Then open out the glued cloth on a fresh sheet of newspaper, lay the left-hand head and fore-edge of the back board up to the pencil mark which will be visible through the glue $\frac{3}{4}''$ from the margins of the cloth, bring the right-hand side of the cloth close and square over the spine hollow and on to the upper board, and smooth all down with the flat of the hand. If French joints are being used run the folding-stick down each side of the spine to form the groove while the glue is soft. Now snip off at an angle of 45°, the four corners of the cloth, making the cut about $\frac{1}{8}''$ from the corner of the boards. The tubular hollow must be slit about $\frac{1}{2}''$ in on either side at head and tail to allow the cloth turn-ins to slide beneath. The turn-ins are done as in making a separate case, doing the fore-edges last and not forgetting to thumbnail in the top and tail protrusions of cloth at the corners. Again run the folding-stick between board and shoulder to make the

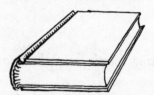

The Deep Joint of French Grooves

French joints deep and sharp, rub the cloth tight over the spine and along all the edges, put the book between boards and leave under a weight to dry.

A simpler method of attaching the boards, so as to be able to make the cover on the book, is to glue a strip along the under spine edge of each board and, having first cut tapes and mull to the required width, smooth them down on the glued surface. Then adjust the position of the boards to give the correct squares and joint spaces, place between pressing boards and leave to dry under a weight. To avoid risk of the glue attaching itself to the waste sheet covering the end-paper, a pressing tin can be laid in either side.

It will now be appreciated that a cloth cover made in the split-board style just described possesses two structural advantages over the separate case. Here the cloth is attached to the spine of the book by the tubular hollow; and the double boards of the case grip the mull and the tapes which are glued in the split. In addition to this when the endpapers are pasted on the inner sides of the cover, the cloth at the joints is forced down to adhere to the mull and, through the mull, to the endpaper, by means of a string of suitable thickness being laid in the French joints (and loosely tied to hold it there) which presses into the joints when the book is screwed down in the press. Thus the split-board cover has a three-point hold on the book while the normal separate case may have only one coat of adhesive to attach mull, tapes and endpapers to the inner surface of the boards. Of course there is no reason why the tubular Oxford hollow should not be used with the case made separately, if extra strength is thought desirable. When this is done no hollow will be used in making the case; the cloth of the case is glued to the Oxford hollow, and left to set, as a preliminary to pasting down the endpapers: in order to get the hollow to slide under the case turn-ins these should be left not glued down, and a $\frac{1}{2}''$ slit made in the folds of the hollow at head and tail. Nor is it uncommon to make the separate case with French joints, indeed there is much to be said for this practice; it adds to the hold between case and book, makes the opening of the book easier, and is now believed to counteract any inclination for the boards to warp.

There is a risk in some school teaching of over emphasizing the importance of strength and durability; a risk of turning the binding into a sort of sarcophagus that will survive the ravages of centuries, yet tend to repel the human touch. The amateur must keep a sense of proportion, and, while learning all he can about split boards and other strength-giving devices, and carefully noting them in the back pages of his notebook, remember to make use of them only when he has to re-bind such books as the family Bible. Cloth bindings come into their own and make the best of themselves when they are light and colourful to the eye and pleasant to the touch. Mention has been made earlier of pin-head squares, cover overlaps that are almost too small for measurement: these go admirably with very small joints, and a board no more substantial than a card, such as folders in a filing cabinet are made of: the cloth should also be thin and of a cambric texture, if such can be found, and the whole finished off with a small leather label pared very thin and neatly tooled in gold. Of course not every book is suited for such delicate treatment, but now and again a little volume of poems may come to hand, or a pocket edition of the Penguin description, even a demy 8vo, if printed on good thin paper; any such book can look supremely happy in a binding attuned to its slender nature. By contrast Faber published in 1937 a little book called *Quia Amore Langueo*, its size is $6'' \times 4\frac{3}{4}''$; its forty pages of hand-made paper bulk only $\frac{1}{8}''$, which is the thickness of each of the heavy boards used in its sea-green cover. The spine is flat, gold lettering down its length, with French grooves to emphasize the joints, all conspiring together to produce a binding beautifully suited to the fourteenth-century poem it encloses. So you never can tell. The amateur should let his imagination roam and avoid as the plague the heavy handed stolidities that can so easily entomb his work if he strives to bind for posterity.

# Half-Binding

As the amateur gains skill and experience he may be tempted, on rare occasions, to add to the gaiety of a binding by making its cover of two different materials or even two colours of the same material. In the trade this is known as quarter-binding if the spine only is different from the sides, but when the four outer corners of the boards are covered with triangular pieces of the material used for the spine— usually leather—then the style is described as half-binding.

Half-binding is a convenient way of making use of the oddments of leather remaining after the skin has yielded whatever full-size covers can be cut from it. Having selected suitable pieces of leather, and a cloth or paper to harmonize with it, the next job is to determine the relative sizes of spine, corners and sides for their proportions to satisfy the eye. The general rule is to make the leather of the spine extend on to the side to one-fifth of the board's width; so that the strip of leather appearing down the side of a book $5\frac{1}{2}''$ wide (demy 8vo) will be just over $1''$ wide, while on a $5''$ book (crown 8vo) it will be just under $1''$. The corners must then be given the same width of leather, measuring from the point of the corner to the centre of the diagonal line of the triangle. In cutting out the leather for spine and corners a $\frac{3}{4}''$ overlap must be added at head and tail to allow for turn-ins, and an extra $\frac{1}{4}''$ given to those edges which go under the material used for sides. All these margins must be pared thin to a point well back from the edges, so that leather and siding material are near enough the same thickness.

The shape and overall size of corners and sides must be worked out by making paper patterns of each, cutting and folding these round the board until turn-ins and overlaps are the right shape to fit into position neatly, and the diagonal lines across the corners are cut to a true 45° angle. The boards should now be marked with pencil guide-lines up to which the various pieces, when glued, are to be laid. Turning in the corner margins will follow the usual procedure, first smoothing over the head (or tail), then tucking in the tiny overlap tucks with the finger-nail, and finally bringing the fore-edge over tight to the board.

Quarter-binding having no corners to complicate the proportions, allows the binder more freedom of choice in the width of material to be shown on the side. This need be no more than will provide a firm hold on the board—say a small ½"—and rarely, if ever, does it look sensible to extend it beyond the conventional one-fifth of the board's width. If a lettering is required on the side, the visually satisfactory placing of it is made easier by keeping the spine overlap to a minimum.

When William Morris had any of his books bound with cloth spines and paper sides he ignored the fractional terminology of the trade and called the style 'Half Holland', as near a plain statement of fact as one may get. The Holland he used was draper's material, buff in colour like unbleached linen, providing at once a pleasing foil for the French grey paper of the sides, a strong hinge for the boards, and a surface rough enough to hold a pasted label. Usually such material needs to be lined with paper before case-making to prevent glue stains coming through. These Half Holland books show beyond a doubt that for this style of binding to look its best the cloth of the spine must be lighter in hue than the paper used on the sides.

Any lettering on the side of a cover needs to be placed slightly left of centre on the board, whether sided or not, to counteract the appearance of extra width given by the joint.

## Pasting the Book into its Case

We now come to that gratifying stage in the proceedings when, having worked through all the operations of constructing, shaping, and strengthening the book, and making a case to fit it, we finally unite the two by pasting down the mull, tapes and endpapers to the under side of the boards, put the finished article in the press with the comfortable reflection that in a few hours' time we shall hold in our hands a bound book.

In pasting down a book the first thing to do is to round the hollow—unless an Oxford hollow is already rounded and in place on the spine of the book. This is best done by gripping both boards and gently shaping the hollow round a short length of metal pipe that has been heated on the stove. Next the mull and tapes must be cut to uniform width, the joints looked to, and any unwanted glue removed. The paste should be thickish, so as not to wet the endpapers more than necessary, and applied with outward moving strokes of the brush to prevent paste getting on the edges. It is now that the importance of the grain of the paper becomes obvious, for unless it runs from head to tail, the endpapers will stretch and wrinkle. When put in the press between pressing boards, the book should not be screwed down hard for ten minutes or so, or the paste may damp through the endpaper. The split-board case made on the book is pasted down in the same way, except that there are no mull or tapes concerned, since they are already glued between the boards. When French grooves have been used a folding-stick should be run down the grooves, to deepen them before laying therein a string of suitable substance and tying it at the tail where the tie will be safely out of the way,

43

then adjusting the pressing boards so that they will force the string down into the joint when screwed in the press.

Sometimes when starting to paste down it is found that the cloth has caused the boards to warp outwardly; this is usually righted by the pull of the endpaper as the paste dries, especially if given a start in the right direction by a little discreet bending. In very obstinate cases the warp can be cured by lining each board before pasting down the book with thin paper pasted into the space between the turn-ins. But always the important thing to remember is to give the hand-bound books a long pressing; at first lightly for a quarter of an hour, then screwed down hard for a while, and finally eased off and left under light pressure until another day. Thus the book becomes flat and firm, and so will remain.

However remote from perfection it may be, the beginner cannot fail to be heartened by a sense of achievement when at last he takes from the press the first book bound by his own hands. He has created something; out of commonplace materials, paper, strawboard, cloth, he has made a book. As he carefully lifts first one cover, then the other, seeing that each opens freely, that endpapers lie smooth and tight to the boards, joints are sharp, squares uniform and so on, he may well feel pleased with his handiwork—pleased, but never quite content. In bookbinding there are so many things to learn, so many subtle gradations of workmanship to be mastered, and always much that remains to be better done next time. Each achievement turns out to be not an end but a revelation of previously unperceived possibilities, a spur to new efforts towards that perfection which is the ultimate goal. It may be that perfection is never wholly attained; it helps if from time to time we glimpse it from afar and so carry in the mind's eye its inspiration.

## Lettering the Cover

All the operations so far described belong to that division of bookbinding which, by old parlance, went under the name of forwarding. As will have been seen the forwarder was in fact the binder of the book, for when it passed from his hands to the finisher who lettered and decorated the cover, the work of binding was complete although in practice, especially when the binding was of leather, the pasting down of endpapers was not done until after the finisher had completed his hand tooled adornments. The amateur should always follow the same procedure for many a book has been ruined by bad tooling, and recovering, if it comes to that, is made more difficult if the endpapers are pasted down.

So we now have to consider that most difficult operation of the bookbinding business, finishing the book with a hand-tooled gold lettering. For our notebook the simplest way of doing this will be to make a little leather label which can be gummed on the spine after the tooling has been successfully accomplished. The professional, of course, would paste the leather in place on the spine of the book and then tool it: in that way he is sure of keeping the tooling sharp and bright. However carefully the label is affixed after it has been gold tooled there is a risk of damp injuring the sharp impressions of the tools. But for the beginner to attempt the tooling with the leather stuck in place is to invite even greater hazards. Indeed one of the best exercises in gold tooling is to make a label or two whenever the opportunity occurs; there is no need to use leather for this purpose, smooth white paper will do just as well, the object being to gain experience in handling the tools and impressing them evenly and straight.

45

One of the attractions of a label is that it can give a touch of contrasting, or complementary colour to the cover, and at the same time add emphasis to the title, so that a quite small type will look suitably strong on a book that would otherwise be too big for it. Any offcuts of leather too small for other purposes, come in useful for labels when pared very thin: the knife must be sharpened to a keen edge and it is advisable to have the leather large enough to be held safely; the label-size piece can be cut out after the tooling has been done, and the edges then shaved away to nothing as a last operation. A useful alternative to this use of odd-ments of leather is the polished skiver known as 'flyswing' which is thin enough for labels without paring. A black fly-swing skiver makes an excellent label for any binding.

Of the tools required for label-making the first essential is a good paring knife. Some workers succeed in honing a satisfactory edge on an ordinary cobbler's knife, but it generally pays to get one that has been specially made for the work with a blade of best steel, such as the French paring knife with a 1½" blade, having the cutting edge across the end, rounded and with a long bevel on the top side. A friendly engineer has been known to make such a knife out of an old unwanted machine-hacksaw blade, teeth ground away, and snapped off to a length of 9" with a curved cutting edge, razor sharp, across its 1¼" wide end. Costing nothing, such a tool is invaluable for paring all sorts of leather and keeps its keen edge with an occasional sharpening on the oil stone and a strop.

Another necessity is a stove for heating hand tools. Dryad Handicrafts make such a stove, with a variable temperature switch and fitted with a serrated rim to support the tools and keep them separate and easy to pick up. This stove costs about £8, a luxury that is very nearly indispens-able: though anyone with a frugal turn of mind may prefer to use the electric boiling ring that heats the glue pot, which

is quite satisfactory for the job, when provided with a support for the handles of the tools. This can be made quite
easily from about four feet of 1″ iron strip, bent to surround

Boiling Ring
& home made stand for tools

the stove at 3″ distance, standing on three legs of suitable
height, fixed in position by rivets. One or two small corks
split half-way help to keep the tools parted into words.
Other items of equipment include a strop made from a
strip of smooth wood, 1′ long and about 2″ wide, covered
with leather, suède side out: a saucer to hold a wet rag for
cooling hot tools: a small roll of ribbon gold.

Lastly, and of prime importance, are the hand tools
needed for lettering the label. There are a number of brass
hand letters and figures in various type faces on the market
and care must be taken in choosing a size and style of letter
suitable for general use. The absence of fine strokes in a
sans-serif type gives a strong clear impression but it is a
stark and rigid type and not to be recommended as a first
choice. Among the best of modern letterings are those made

by Whileys, the goldbeaters. Their York type is an excellent face resembling Eric Gill's Perpetua, cut clean and deep to give a sharp impression and making the delicate art of sighting as simple as possible. The 8 point size of type will be found most generally useful, suiting both title and author's name quite satisfactorily: a set of 39 pieces, figures and punctuation marks will cost about £12. In order to give the label a gold line around the edges a set of pallets will be required, hand tools resembling brass chisels of various widths and costing about £1 10s. od. for a set of four from Dryad.

```
THE TITLE
OF THE
BOOK
o
AN
AUTHOR
```

When preparing to tool a lettering the first thing to do is to pick out the letters required and arrange them in separate words around the heating stove, but without switching on the heat. Then on a sheet of paper draw a pencil line and make a blind impression of the letters of each word, placing the top of each letter right up to this line and keeping the space between letters as even as possible. Several impressions of each word will have to be made until a really well-spaced lettering has been produced: this is important because the object of the exercise is to discover the exact width of the words so that the space each will occupy on the label can be marked on the gold. A piece of ribbon gold of suitable size must now be cut and fixed, bright side up, on a sheet of smooth paper with tiny slips of cellotape at three corners—one corner is left unfixed so that a peep may be taken to see if a good impression has been made. Now with set-square straight-edge and a needle, lightly scratch the correct outline of the label, taking care that all lines are at right angles with each other and clearly visible: then draw another line down the exact centre between the verticals. Across this centre line, a horizontal line for each word of title and author's name must be scratched.

Some discretion is needed in deciding the right position for these title and author lines, bearing in mind that the tops of the letters will be laid up to them: each line of type can be separated by a space equal to the height of the letters, but this depends on the number of words in the title; a two-line title will require a wider spacing than one of four lines. Title and author should be separated by a gap about three times as wide as that between the words: the space between the top of the label and the title should be noticeably less than that between author and bottom of the label. In general the object of spacing is to render the words easy to read and to form a pleasing type pattern when tooled.

The lines to be scratched across the centre line will therefore have to be two letter heights apart, that is one letter height for the word and one for the space: likewise the distance between the last line of the title and the author's name will be four letters: one for the last word and three for the space. When these lines are marked on the gold ribbon a mark must be made on each showing the width of the word to be tooled under it. This is done by halving with dividers the width of each word, as ascertained by the method indicated above, and then marking this half-way point on either side of the central line and just below the cross line up to which the letters are to be tooled.

While this marking up of word widths, etc., is proceeding the heat can be switched on so that the tools will be ready for use when the preliminaries are completed. As each tool is taken from the stove, it is lightly touched on the wet rag in the saucer until it ceases to sizzle, glanced at to see it is right way up, and sighted down its top edge (marked by a notch) on to the cross line. The whole operation must be done as rapidly as possible to avoid losing heat, and the impression made firmly, with a slight rocking movement, and then lifted instantly. The correct way of holding the tool is by gripping it with the fingers of the right hand, thumb on the top, sighting down the upper face of the tool to see that it falls straight down to its mark, being steadied and guided thereto by the thumbnail of the left hand.

Tooling a lettering with all the letters straight and even is one of the most difficult operations in bookbinding. Long and patient practice is required and much gold ribbon and other materials will go into the waste-paper basket before proficiency is attained. For this reason it is recommended that all the preliminary exercises should be done on paper rather than on leather. In this way the proper way of holding the tool and sighting it on to the mark, the right heat, and the speed needed to make the impression before the heat is lost, all these things can be learnt without spoiling anything more valuable than a few sheets of paper and a foot or two of ribbon gold. Every lettering worked with care, and then discarded if unworthy; every tool put down firmly, tight to the guide line, rocked and lifted instantly, is helping to build up that confidence and sureness of touch which at last will produce the straight line of letters, all evenly spaced and impressed. Perhaps not one in a hundred amateur binders ever achieve this, but the student may hearten himself with the reflection that exact uniformity is not his final objective —that can be left to the machine—he strives for it only so that one day he may produce work alive with the light and shade, the controlled freedom, that is the beauty of hand tooling.

When at last the beginner's efforts are rewarded by a reasonably satisfactory label tooled on paper, he can turn his

attention to leather. Here again he is likely to have many
failures before he succeeds in getting all the letters of all the
words properly impressed. It is advisable to keep the gold
stuck to the leather by cellotape at three corners until a peep
under the loose side shows that all is well. By keeping the
gold ribbon in position it is possible to repair a faulty letter
by slipping a new bit of gold beneath the original piece and
then retooling any imperfect letter through the first impression. The lines surrounding the label should be tooled
with the aid of a set square, laying the pallet against it so as
to get a gold line square with each other and with lettering.
Some care is required in sticking the label in position on the
book; a mixture of paste and glue or seccotine should be
used, applied very thin and lightly to avoid making the
leather wet: by measuring and marking the place where it is
to go, a little adhesive can be painted on to the cover to help
in fixing it securely, the label must be placed in position
with the least possible handling and gently smoothed down
while covered by paper. The important points to remember
are to use as little adhesive on the leather as possible to
avoid spoiling it by damp, and to smooth it down no more
than is absolutely necessary.

When all these things have been done successfully and a
nice leather label is securely in place on the spine, the binding of our notebook is finished, and much useful knowledge
and experience will have been gained.

# Re-binding Old Books

---◦◦◦◦◦◦◦---

Having now worked through all the main processes of bookbinding, the next step is to hunt out some job that will bring into use, and perhaps extend, the knowledge and experience already gained. Such a job might well be the re-binding of a book that has become dilapidated through long use, preferably one that is not too big, of no great value and needs an entirely new cover. No one gets much pleasure out of re-binding old books, the result rarely arouses enthusiasm, but the work does give the beginner much useful practice and prepares him to deal with the bundles of tattered leaves that misguided friends will plague him with later on.

Old books are liable to imperfections such as torn or missing pages and plates so it is wise to get into the habit of checking the contents before starting work. If the book belongs to someone else it saves argument to point out its short-comings before it is pulled to pieces. Another matter that should be settled beforehand is whether the cover has any value, either sentimental or otherwise; a first edition, for instance, loses its worth if put into a new case. An inscription inside the cover cannot be saved unless the end-paper on which it is written happens to have been glued down, when it can be damped and then steamed off: if, however, it has been pasted down, as is often the case, it can only be lifted by soaking, which will cause staining from the cloth turn-ins and is rarely worth attempting.

Re-binding starts with doing all the binding operations in

reverse order. First the cover is removed, then the spine is stripped of its mull and brown paper linings, the rounding and jointing are knocked flat, the sewing stitches cut and each section then carefully parted from its neighbour, until the book is again a little pile of separate sections.

The cover can best be removed, as a rule, by holding the book flat on the table with one hand while with the other the board and fly-leaf are gripped and firmly and gently pulled back so as to detach the endpaper along the joint, first on one side and then on the other. In the narrow gap thus made the mull and tapes are exposed and can be slit with a knife to allow the separated cover to be put aside for future attention if required.

Separating the sections is helped by first removing as much as possible of the linings and the glue—rarely an easy matter and one requiring care to avoid damaging the spine folds. Sometimes their linings can be loosened by knocking out the round and the joints, but when the old glue proves very tenacious it may be necessary to damp it with a wet rag or coat it with thin paste for a few minutes' soak, but as this makes the job messy it should be used only as a last resort.

When as much as possible of linings and glue have been removed each section in turn is opened at its centre and its stitches cut—machine sewing has a double thread in all but the first section—so that it can be pulled away or eased off with the help of a thin folding-stick. After separating all the sections in this way, each one will be found to have glue still sticking here and there which must be cleaned off with a knife. This process of splitting an old book into sections and cleaning off fragments of glue, makes a litter of threads, etc., so it is best done over a wide newspaper.

The sections must now be examined for tears and weak places and, where necessary, strengthened with a narrow guard of thin paper pasted and wrapped round the fold. Guards should go inside the fold and it is very desirable to use the fewest possible or the spine will become too fat, and make the appearance of the book wedge shaped and ugly. New endpapers can now be folded and edged-on with paste to the first and last sections. The book should then be knocked-up square and left under a weight for any pastings to dry: when dry it helps to flatten any swelling in the book, as well as the old joint creases, if strawboards of suitable size are laid between every three or four sections and then the whole book is screwed down in the press for a few hours.

Re-sewing, and again gluing, rounding, jointing and lining the spine, will all follow the procedure already described. Old books need a lot of knocking-up at all stages before gluing, since creased leaves are usually reluctant to return to uniformity. Cutting the edges a second time should be avoided, it so easily ruins the page margins. Whenever possible edges should be sandpapered clean and smooth while the book is in an unrounded state.

A new case is always more satisfactory for a re-bound book than trying to renovate an old one: a smart cover distracts attention from any shortcomings inside and provides useful practice in case-making and tooling, whereas repairing a dilapidated case is a tiresome business which rarely looks worth all the trouble taken. The most common failure in an old cover is broken joints that leave the boards and spine hanging precariously together.

Repair involves rejoining the boards with a new strip of cloth inserted under the old cloth on each side to a depth of about $\frac{1}{2}''$, and neatly glued there. Ragged cloth along the joints of the old boards must be cleanly trimmed away, and, as in making the separate case, a spacer strip of strawboard, as wide as the hollow plus $\frac{1}{4}''$ for the spaces, laid between to ensure the boards being the correct distance apart. The two lifted strips of old cloth must then be bent back and glued, and the new cloth, cut $1''$ longer than the board height and wide enough to lay under each upturned flap, is glued on its underside, laid in position and the flaps glued and smoothed down over its edges. The hollow is then laid in position and the head and tail turn-ins completed. The case is then put between pressing boards and left to set in the press. If the old spine is worth keeping it can be trimmed as neat as possible and glued to the new cloth spine after the book has been pasted down and pressed.

## Re-binding Old Leather Books

The re-binding of a leather-bound book follows much the same procedure as when the cover is of cloth, though it is often a more difficult business. Here, too, it is invariably the joints that have failed, leaving the boards loose and the spine detached unless the book has been given a tight back, that is with the spine of the cover glued or pasted direct on to the spine of the book. Tight backs on old books can give that trade term an evil significance when iron-hard glue make it difficult, if not impossible, to detach the leather intact. If the joints have perished the leather of the spine is probably in like condition so that however gently a thin folding-stick or knife strives to ease it away from the book the chances are that it breaks into fragments. Perhaps with special efforts the title section may be removed in usable condition, and this when cleaned on the underside and sandpapered thin around the edges can be squared up to form a label for the new cover, thus preserving a memento of the book's original appearance.

The remainder of the work of reducing a leather-bound book to separate sections will follow the procedure suggested for a cloth-covered book, if, in fact, sewing is really necessary, but so many old books appear to have become dilapidated not from excessive use but because of age and inferior leather. When this is so the original sewing may well be in good condition, so it would be unwise to interfere with it and upset the slick appearance of edges in doing so: all that will be required for re-binding will be new endpapers pasted on, an Oxford hollow made on the spine and a new cover. Possibly, also, the original boards may be in good enough shape to be brought back into service with a new leather spine glued to the hollow and its edges slipped under a lifted flange of the leather on the boards, in the way suggested for repairing broken covers.

It will be appreciated, of course, that this method means the boards cannot be laced to the sewing-cords (unless, perchance, the old boards are still attached and can be used) so the new binding becomes a cased job; but with mull under a strong Oxford hollow this need not cause great concern. The amateur is entitled to avail himself of any short cuts that will ease the thankless job of re-binding, the chief merit of which is that it gives him useful practice in handling the tools and materials of the trade and helps to an understanding of some of the problems of a binder.

The questions that will arise when re-sewing cannot be avoided, whether to sew flexible or sawn-in cords, the sort of endpaper to be used, and many other important details can best be settled if we now consider the whole subject of binding in leather.

# Binding in Leather

**B**efore proceeding very far with the preliminary operations of binding a book in leather, it is important to have a fairly clear picture of the main features of its final appearance. The spine of the bound book, for instance, will probably have the usual five raised bands spaced out down its length. Are these raised bands to be formed by moulding the leather over the actual sewing-cords? If so, the book must be sewn 'flexibly', the stitches being looped round each cord as it stands in its proper place above the level of the spine, and, when it comes to covering, the leather will be stuck direct on to the spine of the book, thus making it what is known as a tight back. This is the traditional method of binding in leather, the way Roger Payne, Cobden Sanderson and the other great masters of the craft did the work, and is the method generally favoured by the pundits. It has the one great disadvantage that every time the book is opened the leather of the spine is creased and this, in time, if the book is much read, injures the gold tooling and produces ugly wrinkles in the leather.

The alternative method now in general use in the trade is to sew with sawn-in cords, line the spine with an Oxford hollow, on to which false bands are glued in the appropriate places. This means that grooves are sawn with a tenon- or hack-saw across the spine folds of the sections, just deep enough to sink the cords flush, so leaving the spine of the book when sewn perfectly smooth for gluing on the tubular hollow. This method of sawing grooves for the bands so as to leave a plain spine surface was in use in

Grolier's time, yet at one period in the distant past it came to
be looked on as an improper practice and a law forbidding
it was enacted by the Guilds with suitable fines for trans-
gressors. The saw-cuts were thought to be damaging to the
spine of the book. However the practice had come to stay,
for the hollow backs had advantages to the binder in the
easier backing of a spine not encumbered with raised cords,
and the speedier sewing provided by saw-cuts, while the
buyer of the book now was able to read it without injury to
the spine and its tooling. These considerations won it
favour until, at last, the old and venerated flexible sewing
became the exception, not the rule.

This then is one of the first questions to be settled, to saw
or not to saw, though the amateur will, of course, wish to
try his hand at both styles of binding. For the first attempt
at a leather-bound book, however, he may well decide to
adopt the sawn-in method. Having reached a conclusion on
the matter of sewing, he must then turn his attention to
endpapers.

## Endpapers

The choice of an endpaper for a leather-bound book requires some deliberation; the paper must be strong enough
for it to perform its part in uniting book and cover, if white
it must match the tone of the text paper, while a coloured
or patterned paper must harmonize with the leather to be
used for the cover. Tradition has always shown a partiality
for 'marble' papers, and in recent years this old practice has
enjoyed a revival due to the wonderful marbling on hand-
made paper done by Sidney Cockerell of Letchworth,
which has provided endpapers for so many of the finest
modern bindings. If, however, a plain undecorated colour

is preferred for the endpaper, the French 'Ingres' papers are admirable for the purpose and can be obtained in a variety of beautiful colours from artists' supply shops, and costing about a shilling a sheet.

Modern commercial practice is to paste the endpaper to the first and last sections before the book is sewn, but the beginner will avoid the danger of stabbing the endpapers with his needle if he attaches them after sewing. Of course the student who is working in a craft school will have been instructed that the endpaper must always be sewn on as an extra section, front and back, if the book is to endure; and since the stitches along the paste-down of an ordinary 8-pp. sewn-on endpaper are considered unsightly, he will have been taught how to make the much favoured 'zigzag' endpaper described in Cockerell's *Bookbinding and the Care of Books*, which ingeniously avoids the disfiguring stitches in the first opening.

Without doubt sewing makes the endpaper an integral part of the book, thus giving it a strength beyond any other method. Nevertheless, this is an unnecessary elaboration on most of the books an amateur will bind, for all of which a perfectly satisfactory endpaper, as simple as it is efficient, is the double or, if the book is small and thin, a single 4 pp. pasted to an overcast first and last section.

The double four-page endpaper is made up of two folded papers insetted to form an 8 pp., the inner being attached to the outer by an edging of paste along the fold, so joining it to the leaf next the book. When this pasting is set, the whole 8 pp. is pasted to an overcast section. The first leaf is the protector to be torn away when binding is finished, page 3 is the paste-down, leaving two fly-leaves on the book. Where a coloured endpaper is required, the inner 4 pp. is coloured paper, the outer 4 pp. white to match the text paper of the book.

## Sewing for Leather Binding

The overcast sewing mentioned above consists of a series of looping stitches made along the spine of the section, so tying together the narrow strip of all the leaves within the hold of the stitches. A guide line is lightly drawn parallel to, and about $\frac{3}{32}''$ from, the spine fold, the first stitch pierces this line $\frac{1}{4}''$ from the tail of the sheet and the cotton drawn through twice and tied: succeeding stitches are made about $\frac{1}{4}''$ apart, the cotton coming from below, up, over, and down again through the sheet, forming a series of loops which end at the head with a double sewing through the same hole and a tie. This overcasting saves all the pull of a pasted end-paper falling on the first leaf of the section, the cotton stitches passing some of it to the other leaves.

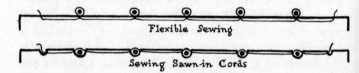

It is usual to sew leather-bound books on five cords or bands, though very thin or small books sometimes look better if sewn on four. The position of these bands must be worked out carefully on paper and then clearly marked in pencil lines drawn across the spine with a set square: the spaces above and below all the bands are the same depth, except the one at the tail which should have slightly more space below it. For sawn-in sewing these pencil lines represent the saw-cuts for the cords, an additional line and cut is required for each kettle-stitch, about $\frac{1}{2}''$ from the head and $\frac{1}{4}''$ from the tail. After marking these lines the book must be knocked-up square at head and spine, placed between strawboards and screwed tight in the lying press, with just enough of the spine showing for the worker to see that the

Marking-up for Sewing Five Cords

saw-cuts are no deeper than the thickness of the cords required. The sawing is done after the book has been given a good nip all over and before endpapers are affixed.

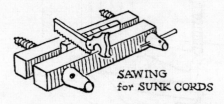

SAWING
for SUNK CORDS

Before starting to sew it is well to check that all sections are in the right order; then place the book near to the left hand, title uppermost and spine towards the worker. Sewing with cords is greatly facilitated by the use of a sewing press, in which they can be stretched tight, vertical, and all in position. The beginner working at home is unlikely to possess that luxury, in which case the cords will have to be spaced out along the edge of a strawboard, and there fixed with cellotape. While the first few sections are being sewn, the cords are likely to flop about but soon they will be held by the stitches and cease to give trouble. The board on which the cords are attached should have another book, or a few pressing boards, placed above it to lift the sewing conveniently clear of the table on which the work is being done.

The sewing will be done in the same way as for tapes, starting at the head and each stitch coming out through the saw-cut, across the cord and in again on the far side of it, through the same hole, so that the thread, when pulled tight at the tail, forces the cords down into their grooves. Care must be taken to press each section, as it is sewn, close down on to its predecessor, otherwise they will tend to ride up the cords and cause gaps that are difficult to correct later.

Sewing flexibly follows the same procedure, except that now the needle is brought out of the sheets on the far side of

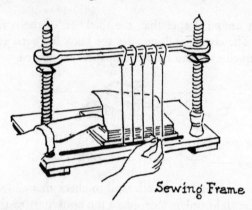

Sewing Frame

each cord, then returns across it, to re-enter on the near side through the same hole. It is important not to let the needle pierce the thread when it is pushed through the hole made where it emerged; it is equally necessary to sew round, and not through, the cord. A final point to watch is to pull each stitch tight, but not to get the kettle-stitch so tight that the book is pinched-in at head and tail. And, lastly, flexible sewing is where the need of a sewing press is felt most acutely, for the cords are riding on the surface of the spine, without saw-cuts to keep them in a straight and narrow path, and crooked cords are the very devil. A simple way out of the difficulty is to punch needle-sized holes in the spine folds of all the sections, using a fine bodkin and guided by a sheet marked with the positions of kettle-stitches and cords, in the manner suggested for sewing with tapes. These holes make sewing easier and, provided that the needle is pushed through the appropriate hole and nowhere else, the cords are kept straight.

## Forwarding

The book is now seen to be taking shape; folding has joined the leaves into sections; sewing has entered each section to hold the inner leaves in place, and, emerging, has clasped each supporting cord in turn, finally weaving a kettle-stitch chain across the spine at head and tail to link all securely together. Sewing, when well done, leaves a little freedom of movement among the sections; it is the function of the glue to act as a bond between them, so completing the unification of the spine, and changing its separate parts into a whole that can be moulded and will retain the desired shape. In modern usage this transformation of sewn sheets into a bound book is known as forwarding.

Before gluing the spine there are one or two preparatory operations to be done. The cord-ends, now often referred to as 'slips', must be unravelled and combed out with a needle or bodkin until they stand out on either side like tresses of golden hair, each about 2″ long. The book is then placed between protecting strawboards, with the cords outside, knocked-up square at head and back, and screwed tight in the lying press, leaving about 1″ of book protruding above the press blocks. Then with knocking-down iron and hammer, first on one side and then on the other, the spine is gently hammered to bring all the sections close and compact, when any rucks that may have appeared in the cords can be pulled out to leave them tight and straight across the spine. The back is now ready for gluing, which is the precise point at which another important decision has to be made. Are the edges to be cut the easy way, while the book is still in a flat condition? Or is that delicate operation to be made more difficult by doing it in the traditional way known as 'cutting-in boards', which means cutting the edges after the book has been rounded, jointed and the boards laced to the sewing cords?

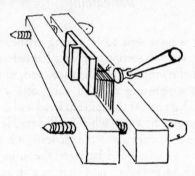

Knocking down sewing swell

The object of cutting *after* the back has been rounded and jointed is that it gives the edges, and especially the fore-edge, a smooth glassy finish that is practically unobtainable by other means. This is most noticeable in old leather-bound books where the edges, cut by the 'inboards' method have the appearance of the polished marble that their decoration seeks to imitate. It is one of the subtle refinements the dedicated bookbinder is always striving after. Rounding and jointing causes a slight starting forward of the leaves, especially at the beginning and end of the book, a movement that may be visible if the rounding is done after cutting. The monks of ancient times, probably using paper of stouter substance that is normal today, noticed this move-

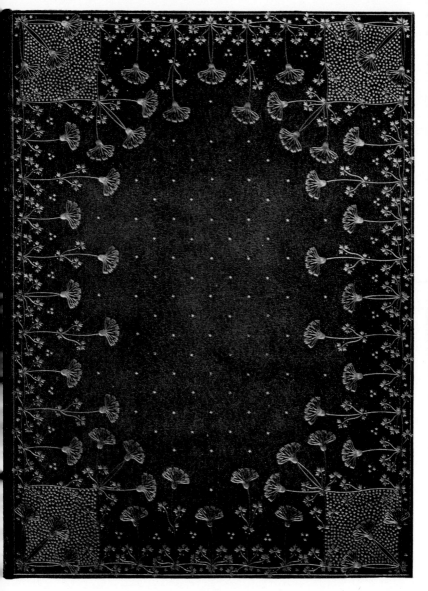

Cobden-Sanderson's Adonais cover design

and the Tools with which he made it

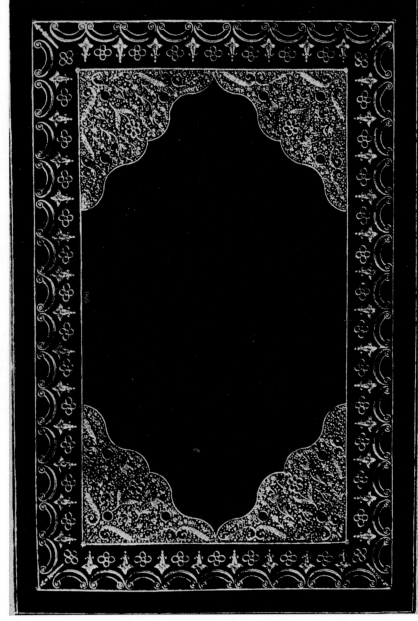

A Roger Payne binding

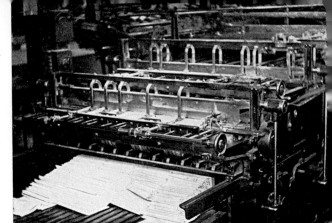

Machine folding a 64-pp. sheet into 4 × 16 pp.

Gathering machine

Sewing-machine mechanism

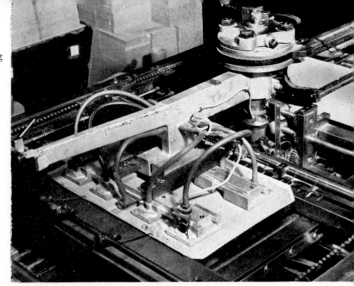

Case-making machine mechanism

Modern blocking press with automatic feed

Backing, lining and casing-in machine linked up to form one unit

ment and invented the method of 'cutting-in boards' to overcome the defect. By cutting the edges after the movement has occurred, when all the leaves are fixed in their final relationship, a perfectly smooth surface is produced.

However, it would be fair to say that most of the books the amateur will bind will be printed on paper that can be backed quite satisfactorily after the edges are cut. Indeed the number of books which are now cut in-boards are few, outside the craft schools. Providing the round of the back is not too great and the jointing done with care, cutting 'out of boards' is a reasonable simplification of the operation.

The choice between the two methods is made now, because in-board work, which is for immediate backing, will have the spine glued with thin hot glue, well rubbed in as the next process after sewing: whereas the book, that is first to be cut, only needs to be tipped up with glue in order that it may retain its knocked-up squareness while the edges are being ploughed.

For both methods the rounding and jointing of the spine will be the procedure already described for the cloth covered book, with which, no doubt, the beginner is now quite familiar. As soon as the glue ceases to be tacky, yet still flexible, the book is laid flat on the paring stone, fore-edge foremost, left hand spread on book, pulling, thumb against fore-edge, pushing, the backing hammer tapping all along the upjutting spine to force the outer sections, first on one side, then on the other, to ride forward evenly. The swell of thread in the back will help this movement, and if the tension of the sewing has been kept fairly uniform, a nice flattish round is not difficult to achieve, though both sides may need more than one going over to obtain a good shape.

The rounded book is at once marked up for backing before the glue gets too dry, a pencil line being drawn parallel to the spine and at a distance from it equal to the thickness of the board (about $\frac{1}{8}''$). The backing boards are then given a touch of the tongue to prevent slipping, laid with their sharp ends tight and even against the line marked, the frayed cords left outside, and the books and boards screwed up in the lying press. This operation requires great care for it is better to do it all again if there is any doubt about the boards being exactly aligned, before the press is tightened.

Forming the joints on a book sewn on cords requires some nicety in the use of the hammer, to avoid flattening or cutting the cords, while ensuring that the joint is properly formed under each. With a flexibly sewn book, where the cords stand above the spine, the flat end of the hammer must be used close in on either side of each cord to get the joints well down on to the descending surface of the backing boards.

When the joints are seen to be evenly formed, and standing at right angles to the surface of the book, the spine must be given a coat of paste and left to soak for a few minutes. Then the paste is cleaned off with a folding-stick and soft paper, till the sections are white again and wet with paste that has soaked in, and the valleys between are full of paste and softened glue which will heal any fractures the backing may have caused, all of which will leave the spine, when dry, stronger and more springy than it was before.

## Cutting the Boards

This is one of the points at which the book should rest undisturbed in the press for several hours, all night if possible, so that the gluing, backing, and the paste of the cleaning off all become set hard and beyond fear of injury in subsequent operations. Meanwhile the boards can be measured, lined and cut. It is best to cut the boards a little larger than required, line them on the inside with thin paper well pasted, and, after nipping them in the press, stand them out to dry, which will cause them to draw towards the lined side.

For leather work a millboard should be used of a substance equal to ·090. These can be roughly cut from the sheet with a good knife and straight-edge, which is hard work, or with the garden shears, taking care that the maker's cut edge is kept as a guide when the boards are cut down to exact size. It is, of course, best if all the cutting can be done on a board chopper, such as is found in schools; though the craftsman would do it with a plough. The home alternative is the mount chopper which calls for some strength and much care in preventing a tendency to twist.

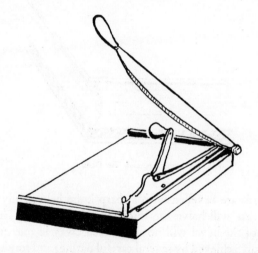

The correct size for the boards to be cut to when the lining is quite dry is the height of the shortest pages in the book, and the width measured by dividers from the joint at the spine to just inside the narrowest leaf. The cutting of the book's edges will provide the necessary overlapping squares on the boards at head, tail and fore-edge.

Sometimes it is a good idea to bevel the boards of a leather-bound book, especially when the book happens to be thin. Very thin books are inclined to look overpowered by the cover boards if the thickness of the two boards together equals, or even exceeds, the width of the book itself. Such books can be given an illusion of greater substance if the boards are bevelled on the inside, so that only a narrow edge of board is to be seen, leaving a chamfered leather margin sloping inwards to the book. If this leather margin is later tooled all round with some simple pattern it provides an attractive gold frame to the book, giving a rich appearance to the work if the edges have been gilt.

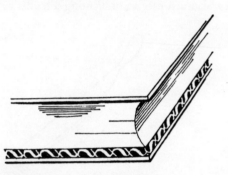

Tooled pattern around Turn-ins

Boards are bevelled with a sharp knife held firmly at an angle that will halve the thickness of the board. The full depth of the bevel will not be shaved away in one go, but gradually achieved by several careful parings and finished off with sandpaper. Boards that are to be bevelled on the inside must first be placed in position for the book size to be marked on them, first with a folding-stick (to save marking the edges) and then with pencil. For inside bevels it is advisable to have the squares wider than normal.

When cut to size the boards must be laid exactly in place,

one at a time, and the position of the cords marked along the spine edge; front and back should also be clearly marked on book and boards. A line is then drawn ½" from the edge of the board, and where the cord mark crosses this line a hole is punched with an awl: a similar row of holes, in line with the first but ¼" further in, is then punched from the inside of the

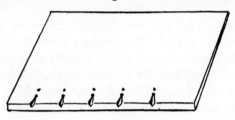

board. Now on the outside again a groove is cut between each hole and the board's edge, just deep enough to sink the cord flush with the surface of the board. Each cord is then pasted, its tip cut square, twisted to a point, and threaded

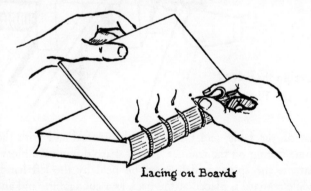

Lacing on Boards

from the outside in; then from the inside out again through the second row of holes, and there cut off flush. When both boards are thus laced on, the knocking-down iron is set in the end of the lying press and on that each cord-end, and the burr around the holes, carefully hammered flat and smooth while the paste in the cord is yet damp. The book is again given a good pressing with tins above and below each board.

## Cutting the Edges

Cutting a book with the plough, whatever may be said by the experts, is a hazardous business, especially when done after it has been rounded. Before the fore-edge can be cut, the round spine must be knocked flat, which is done by placing a pair of trindles (metal objects resembling the button sticks used by soldiers) between the boards, which are

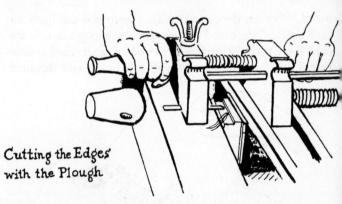

Cutting the Edges
with the Plough

flat on the table, and the book held vertical and with the spine resting on the trindles. A few sharp downward blows flattens the spine, which must be held by the left hand, while a board is placed at the back as a cut against, and another board laid to a previously pencilled line at the front. Book and cutting boards are then lowered into the lying press, the trindles being removed, while all are held square with the cutting line exactly flush with the surface of the press.

Before any of these things are done, the plough knife has been ground to a keen edge on the oil stone, and tested in position to see that it moves across the gap in the lying press in a true horizontal line, and when the book is successfully in the press, the plough knife should again be tested to ensure its movement following exactly the guide line marked on the endpaper. When all is in order the plough is worked evenly back and forth, with a downward pressure, and a slight inward turn of the screw after each cut. It is important to work with deliberation: too hasty cutting may jag the paper. The round returns to the spine as soon as the book is released from the press, helped, if need be, by a wriggle with the hand around the spine and a crooked finger against the fore-edge.

In cutting the head and tail the book is put in the lying press, back towards the worker, the right-hand board lowered a square to show the amount to be cut off, and a sheet or two of waste, or thin strawboard, placed between the book and the left-hand board, to save it being cut.

## Gilding the Edges

Gilding the edges of a book is a highly specialized business and rare indeed is the amateur who succeeds in doing it well: usually it is much better to give the job to a professional who, for a few shillings, will produce a gilt edge that is good to look on. The charge for gilding all three edges is about 7s. 6d.

The leaves are first fanned out and dusted with French chalk along the edge to be gilt: the book is then placed between boards flush with the edge, screwed tight and square in the lying press and scraped with a scraper to remove inequalities and finger-prints. Now the gold leaf is cut to size, rather wider than needed, using a gold cushion and a knife rubbed clean of grease and finger-marks: the cut gold is picked up on squares of paper, which have been first touched on the hair or cheek, and laid ready for use. The edge is then painted with a paste made of blacklead and glair, and brushed with a boot brush till it shines like the kitchen stove: on that surface thin glair is then painted with a camel-hair paint brush and left to dry a moment. Next an area little bigger than one strip of the cut gold, is flooded with glair, the gold on its paper brought close until it is drawn down to the glair without the paper actually making contact. When the whole edge is covered with gold leaf in this way it is left about an hour to dry. The time to begin burnishing is when the mist caused by breathing on the gold vanishes immediately. Before applying the burnisher direct, the gold should be rubbed down by using the burnisher through a sheet of hard, smooth paper, and then lightly touched all over with a beeswaxed leather. The crux of the matter is in the blind discovery of that intangible moment when the glaired gold is at its prime for burnishing: taken too early the gold will push off to leave dirty streaks: too late and it flakes to powder.

As an alternative to gilding, and specially suitable for cloth work, the top can be coloured, using water colour mixed with glair or very thin paste. This can be painted on with a broad brush, and then brushed till it shines, with a boot brush that has been slightly rubbed on the beeswax.

## Headbands

The main function of a headband is decorative, though it also gives support to the leather headcap of the spine. It consists of a strip of leather, string or hardboard as a foundation, covered by a binding of silk thread in one or two colours. The height of the foundation should be slightly less than the width of the squares. For a two-colour headband, about a foot of silk thread of each colour is knotted together in one length with the needle threaded and tied at one end. The book is set up in the press (or the plough with the knife removed), held by one corner with the top edge sloping away from the worker and in a good light. The needle is pushed through the middle of the first section to come out just below the kettle-stitch, the thread pulled through up to the joining knot, brought up from the back and over, and again passed through the same hole, so forming a loop

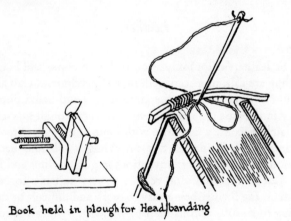

Book held in plough for Head/banding

through which the thong foundation is then passed to leave a small overlap beyond, the thread is then drawn tight and again brought up and over, and beneath the thong to en- circle the first loop and hold it secure. This needle thread is then allowed to fall to one side and the second thread passed over the first thread and under the thong and up and over it twice. The thong is now covered by a double loop of each colour. As one colour is dropped and the second brought over it to make its two loops, a beading begins to form in front of and at the base of the headband. This beading can be accentuated by twisting the threads together, once only, at each change of colour. From time to time the needle thread is again passed down between the leaves and out below the kettle-stitch to hold down the headband close to the book. This process is repeated until the whole of the headband has been worked to the full extent of the spine. When again, as at the beginning, a double tie down is made through one hole, and both threads are knotted at the back and there pasted down as close and neat as possible.

## Leather

The leathers commonly associated with books and book-binding are calf, morocco, vellum, and parchment. Calf and vellum both come from the same animal and had a popularity in the past they do not enjoy today; though box-calf has lately become a favourite with some of the great French binders, its sleek, flat surface providing a splendid background for their modern inventions in gold tooling and inlay. But neither calf nor vellum is very suitable for the amateur, the former being easy to mark and difficult to tool owing to its soft, porous nature: while the vellum requires skilful handling and is affected by atmospheric changes and is liable to warp. Parchment is usually a split sheepskin and its transparency makes a paper lining necessary. Sheepskin goes under many names, basil, roan, skiver and others, all of which are used in commercial binding but have nothing to recommend them to the amateur.

In the past sheepskin and calf earned a bad reputation for fragility; many ornate Victorian bindings, showing little sign of wear, were found to have broken at the joints, leaving boards and spine detached with the leather flaking and brittle. In 1900 the Royal Society of Arts appointed a committee of experts to investigate the causes of this decay and among their findings was this comment on grained sheepskin:

'Sheepskins are grained in imitation of other leathers, and these imitation-grained leathers are generally found to be in worse condition than any of the other bindings except, perhaps, some of the very thin calfskins.'

More recent investigations have shown that the chief cause of decay in these leathers was due to the presence of sulphuric acid, which it was found could be absorbed from the atmosphere by vegetable tanned leathers. An interesting account of the experiments which led to this discovery, and the means devised to combat the damage caused by sulphuric acid is contained in Plenderleith's *The Preservation of Leather Bookbindings*, a British Museum publication.

Some of the failure of those old books was, however, due to the paper-thin leather used by the binders. Thin leather greatly facilitates the work of the binder; it reduces the need for much paring and makes covering a neater job. Sooner or later every amateur finds out for himself the difficulties inherent in thickish leathers, especially in binding thin books. A narrow spine affords so small a surface for the leather to hold to that there is always a danger that it may pull away when the boards are opened after the book has been covered, thick leather being unwilling to make the close 'Z' fold that a thin spine requires. This danger should, of course, be foreseen and a certain amount of paring done all along both joints to render that part of the cover more flexible. Even so, the leather may still tend to pull away from the book, and when this happens it can usually be cured by opening each side in turn and working a little strong hot glue down between the cords and on to the spine with the help of a small paintbrush. The spine must then be well rubbed down, with the boards closed, left several hours to dry hard, and when opened the movement must be slow and gradual, pressing the board down into the joint all the time to prevent it putting a strain on the spine.

Morocco, providing it is genuine goat, and not a sheepskin imitation, is the best leather for the amateur. There are a variety of moroccos to choose from, Levant, straight grain, hard grain and others, but the leather which has most to recommend it to the beginner is Oasis Niger morocco, which has a beautiful, natural grain, is dyed in many colours, is easy to work and pares well. It is advisable to choose a thin skin that will require as little paring as possible, and one free of the small blemishes Niger is liable to, where the goat has scratched himself on a thorn bush.

## Cutting and Paring the Cover

Before cutting out the cover it is well to make a paper pattern of the size required, allowing ¾" extra all round for turn-ins, and with that as a guide, select that part of the skin best suited to the job, and where it cuts out most economically. When the cover is cut, the position of boards and spine must be marked in pencil as a guide when paring.

The paring knife should be sharpened with oil stone and strop until it has a razor edge; a little extra trouble in this matter saves much labour in paring. The paring cuts are made with the knife held flat and fingers pressing down, starting just inside the pencil line and gradually thinning the leather away to nothing at the edge. Paring must be kept as even as possible all around the turn-ins, testing it from time to time to see when the leather is thin enough to turn easily, and to discover harsh points that require extra attention. On thin books it may be necessary to do a very little paring

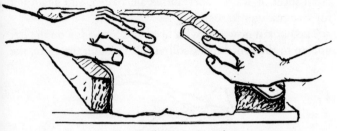

Paring the Leather

along the joints as mentioned earlier to allow the boards to open freely.

## Covering

One or two points require attention before pasting the cover. If the spine is lined with a tubular hollow, false bands either of leather, cord or suitable board must be cut and glued into position, and each corner of the hollow slit down $\frac{1}{4}''$ in the joint to receive the turn-ins: from the inner corner of each board, beside the headband, a small tapering sliver is cut away, wider on the surface than below, to ease the movement of the board where the turn-in doubles the thickness of the leather: the cords, where they lie in little grooves cut in the board, should have paste put behind them: and the sharp corner of each board given a very slight round. Gilt edges must be protected by a close-fitting paper wrapping on all three sides.

The surface of the leather should now be damped all over on the outside to prevent moisture from the paste staining through, the inner side well pasted with paste as thick as thick cream, and the cover folded paste to paste and left to soak for a short time. The leather is then opened out on a

77

clean sheet of waste paper and again pasted, and again left for five minutes to soak.

The book is now laid with head and fore-edge on the left side up to the pencil mark still visible through the paste, the

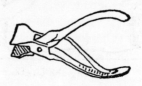

leather brought round over the spine and on to the upper board, and smoothed down over all. Then, with margins turned out, the book is stood up on its fore-edge for the leather on the spine to be worked up around the bands, and

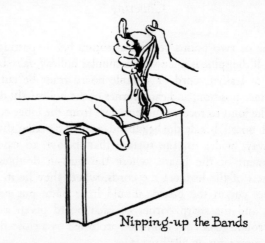

Nipping-up the Bands

smoothed down between, so that the raised bands look worthy of their name, and stand out boldly. In this a pair of band nippers are of great value, giving a two-sided pressure to the band and forcing down the leather at its base. At this time also a bibbed apron is useful as protection from waistcoat buttons, for the wet leather is easily marked by that sort of thing: a ring, or pointed finger-nail, is another source of danger.

All the operations of covering must be done as rapidly as may be, for the damp of paste which renders leather mouldable soon evaporates. Having gone over the spine and bands, the margins at head and tail must be turned in, putting a fresh touch of paste on the margins above the spine before sliding it smoothly down under the lip of the hollow, and flattening it there with the folding-stick.

The fore-edges are turned in last: then the corners, one at a time, are lifted, spread flat on the stone and cut off at an angle of 45°. With a sharp knife the cut edge is bevelled off to nothing, pasted, turned in again at top, then at fore-edge with the least possible tuck inside it, and the whole rubbed down smooth with a folding-stick. In making the fore-edge turn-in the leather must be made to take a true mitre line from the corner inside the board.

When all four corners are completed in this way, each board is opened right back and pushed forward firmly against a square-edged pressing board laid close in to the joint. This helps to get the cover board set true with the angle of the joint. Now the top and tail corners of each joint, between spine and board, is clearly defined with a folding-stick and a loop of thread tied tight in the marks so made, and a knot tied at the tail where it cannot mark the leather. A thin folding-stick is then slid down the spine, between leather and book, to force out the leather against the restraint of the thread and also to draw up sufficient leather to form a head-cap over the headband: an operation which is completed by rubbing it down against the flat paring stone. When the head-caps are made, all the bands and the spaces between must be worked over again, the turn-ins and board edges smoothed over, the whole cover looked at for the last minute attentions and, finally, a pressing tin, safely enclosed

79

in a folded sheet of grease-proof paper laid inside both boards and the book left to dry with clean blotting-paper above and below, and all covered by a board and a weight just heavy enough to prevent warping. Wet leather is easily stained by the touch of metal, so pressing tins must be entirely covered, and the band nippers electroplated. The book should be left to dry for at least twenty-four hours: it does no harm to look to see that all is well occasionally, gently pressing home the spine leather and smoothing down, but not opening the boards lest the hold of the leather on the back be disturbed. When quite dry, the turn-in margins should be cut square all round and the centre space filled in with paper cut to size and pasted to provide a surface flush with the leather of the turn-ins on which the endpaper will be pasted down after the cover has been tooled.

## Finishing

Finishing, the art of lettering and decorating the cover of a book by means of gold leaf and hand tools, is the most difficult part of bookbinding, yet, like the other operations, in essence it is simple. A blind impression of the lettering or design required is made on the leather with warm tools, this is given two coats of glair, gold leaf is laid on, and the lettering or design again tooled with hot tools: surplus gold is then cleaned off with a greasy rag or rubber, leaving a gilt impression of the tools worked. The art of the matter lies in choosing the moment when the glair is not too dry to be effective nor still damp enough to dull the gold: in gauging the right heat for the tools, and in making each impression in line with the others, upright, and of uniform depth.

Glair is made of half a teaspoonful of albumen crystals in half a cup of hot water which, when dissolved and strained through muslin, produces a liquid of the consistency of milk, and should be kept in a screw-topped bottle. For cutting gold leaf to size, a gold cushion can be made from a piece of wood 6" × 4" padded with cotton wool and covered with a waste piece of leather, rough side out. It is useful to dust this with brickdust to prevent the gold adhering. Cotton wool, a small pot of vaseline, a fine paint brush, and a saucer containing a wet rag are the sundries required.

Mention was made earlier of Whiley's 8-point York hand letters as being an excellent type face and size for general use. These letters can be made to serve most of the beginner's requirements for, although it is normal practice to use a larger type for the title than for the author's name, this is by no means essential. Prominence can be given to the title by spacing the letters, enclosing the words in a panel, making a label of a different colour from the leather of the cover, or even by the use of lines between the words. Where the spine is divided up by raised bands, a blank panel can be left between the title and the author, the title being tooled in the second and the author in the fourth panel from the top, an arrangement which makes the same size of type for both perfectly acceptable. However, if at any time a need is felt for a larger, or smaller lettering, York hand letters are made in several sizes.

The tools used by the finisher for the basic elements of decoration, the straight line and the curve, are known as pallets, fillets, and gouges. Pallets are used for short lines across the spine of a book, or for making panels or labels, and are made in sets of various lengths: the fillet is a brass wheel set in a wooden handle by which the longer lines required on the sides of covers can be rolled: it has a gap cut in its circumference for convenience in joining the corners of a frame. Gouges are segments of a circle, resembling the curved chisels used by carpenters, and their use is the formation of curves such as are seen in the geometrical patterns on

F
81

a Grolier binding: with gouges the skilled finisher can tool circles, ovals, and almost any curve the design may require.

Another tool very popular in the past, but rarely seen to-day, is the Roll, a brass wheel with a continuous pattern engraved around its edge, with which a ribbon of ornament was rolled on to the sides of the cover, usually as an elaborate

THE COMMENTARIES OF EUTHYMIUS. PRINTED IN 1550.
*Bound for Jean Grolier.*

frame around the margins; sometimes more than one ornamental roll would be used in conjunction with the straight
lines of fillets, one within the other, so building up a
specially rich framework to enhance the beauty of the main
design, as may be seen in some of Samuel Mearne's 'Cottage'
bindings. The roll was one of the earliest mechanical devices
for easing the labour of covering large areas with intricate
gold tooling. The cost of engraving would have made the
roll part of a binder's general equipment to be employed on
any suitable book; so the connoisseur seeking an exclusive
design would regard them with disfavour: their use was
also liable to the blemish of doubling the impression where
vertical and horizontal ribbons of pattern met and over-
lapped. The amateur who wishes to decorate his work with
an ornamental frame would do better to follow the example
of the great eighteenth-century English binder, Roger
Payne, whose bindings are often enriched with elegant
borders formed by repeated impressions of one or two small
hand tools, always peculiarly his own, and which he himself
is said to have engraved. Patterns evenly unrolling from an
engraved roll are likely to have the rather flat surface produced by a block, whereas a design formed by numerous
impressions of small tools cannot fail to be alive with the
light and shade caused by those inequalities of depth and
angle which are the charm of hand work.

When starting to tool any lettering or design it is essential
to work it out on paper so as to get all the measurements
right and ensure that it will fit the available space. The procedure for setting out a spine lettering has already been described. The first thing is to ascertain the length of each word,
then draw a series of horizontal lines one above the other
spaced two letters apart: across these two vertical lines are
ruled to show the width of the spine, with a third line between to give the exact centre: the word widths are then
ticked off on each horizontal line using the centre line as the

half-way point of every word. A good black impression of hand tools, for these experiments on paper, can be obtained by warming the tools and then touching them on carbon paper. When a satisfactory layout of lettering or design has been finally achieved, it can be cut out and fixed in position on the cover with a snippet of cellotape, to serve as a guide for a blind impression to be made with hot tools through the paper on to the leather. Some care is required in placing the pattern straight and true: for a spine lettering it helps if a dot is lightly marked on the side of the raised bands exactly in the middle above and below the panel to be lettered; you then align the centre line of the pattern on those. Before re-moving the paper it is useful to get into the habit of lifting a corner, without disturbing its position, to see if the letters are impressed clearly enough, and then blind all in again directly on to the leather. When all the letters are distinct, and any crooked ones twisted straight, the impressions can be neatly painted with glair, using a fine brush to avoid spreading glair where it is not wanted. In ten minutes' time this will probably be dry enough to receive a second coat of glair, and that may require an hour before it is sufficiently dry for tooling to commence.

Meanwhile a sheet of gold can be laid out on the cushion and cut to size with a knife wiped clean of finger-marks. A wet rag in a saucer for cooling the tools, a small pad of cotton wool to wipe the blind impressions with vaseline, a slightly larger pad for lifting the gold from cushion to cover (and an unpowdered cheek to wipe it on first)—when all these are ready, and the tools given a polish on the rough side of a piece of leather as they are set out around the stove, then the great moment has arrived, the gold can be laid on and tooling begun.

The vaseline pad is lightly rubbed on the whole panel, care being taken to get it into all the impressions to hold the gold down and make the letters clear to see. Then the gold pad is drawn across the cheek or hair, the gold lifted from the cushion and pressed into position: if any breaks appear, a second piece of gold is laid on, breathing on the first to get the second to adhere.

Choosing the right moment to begin tooling, and the right heat for the tools, is never an easy matter, and the beginner will be helped in discovering it if he has by him a waste piece of leather with a few impressions of tools prepared in exactly the same way as on the book, and at the same time, with which he can first make a trial tooling, and, when that proves successful, commence the main work. If the gold appears dull and frosty the glair may be insufficiently dry or the tool too hot. The tool should be touched on the wet rag and used the moment it ceases to hiss, holding it with the fingers of the right hand, thumb on top, and sighting vertically down the notched top side. Speed is essential if the heat is not to be lost; the tool should be planted firmly in the blind impression which is seen through the gold, rocked slightly with an upward tendency, and instantly lifted.

When all the words have been tooled in this way the surplus gold can be cleaned off with a greasy rag: any imperfect letters will have to be pencilled in with glair, laid on with fresh gold, and tooled a second time. And lucky indeed is the amateur who succeeds with the first attempt. There are so many intangible factors in gold tooling, the glair, the heat, the touch, all have their secrets, and only after much striving and many failures does an instinct, a blind comprehension, begin to enlighten the head and hand of the devoted worker.

The best work is, and always has been, done in the manner just described, but today ribbon gold provides an efficient and simpler means of gold tooling the covers of books. It eliminates the preliminary blinding-in, the use of glair and vaseline, and the laying on of gold leaf; and in their place substitutes a thin cellophane ribbon carrying on its under-side real gold in powder form, covered with the necessary adhesive to fix the gold when impressed by heated tools. In general less heat is required for working with ribbon gold than with gold leaf and glaire. Indeed the tendency for the cellophane ribbon to spread the heat of the tools, so blurring the outline and perhaps filling in enclosed spaces like the loops as such letters as 'P' and 'B', makes it important to work with tools as cool as practicable; and that is something only to be discovered by experiment. But by eliminating glair wash from gold tooling, ribbon gold has removed one of the chief enigmas that harass the beginner; there is no invisible damp in the leather to spoil his best endeavours and so he is left free to puzzle out for himself the right heat for the work.

Ribbon gold requires the same preparatory work for measuring the width of the words and arriving at a satis-factory layout for the lettering, all of which must be done on paper; when that has been achieved only the guide lines and word widths need be lightly scratched with a needle on the cellophane, which is then carefully fixed in position, and the tooling done direct on to it in the normal way. When all the words have been tooled in, it is necessary to peep be-neath the cellophane, without shifting more than a corner at a time, to see that all letters have been properly impressed on the leather. If the cellophane remains in its original position it is sometimes possible to repair a faulty letter by re-tooling through the original impression: this saves the troublesome business of trying to make good a weak letter by partly covering it with a new piece of gold and re-tooling half at a time, leaving exposed just enough of the letter for sighting purposes.

Tooling patterns and ornaments with ribbon gold follows the same procedure, the design being carefully worked out on paper to get all measurements right, and then just the essential guide lines are scratched on the cellophane. Guide lines should always be made for the head of the tool, not the tail, to be laid up to, for in that way the tool is given an inclination slightly forward from the vertical, so making an

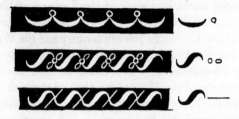

Borders made with simple tools

impression that is more likely to reflect light than one made with a downward trend. Since cellophane has a slippery surface to work on, the tool must be held and impressed firmly, the base of the brass shaft being steadied with the left thumbnail.

## The Use of Ornament

Every amateur feels the urge to enrich his work with decoration of his own devising, for however beautiful may be the natural graining of the unadorned leather, it is the gold tooling of an original design that makes it something peculiarly his own, and on rare occasions may transform it into a work of art. All the great bindings preserved in the world's museums and libraries are there because the ornamentation with which some inspired workmen have embellished their covers. Decoration is the culminating achievement of the bookbinder, the supreme operation for which all that has gone before is but the preparation.

Perhaps this traditional elaboration of book covers owes
something to the religious zeal of the monastic binders who,
centuries before the art of gold tooling came to Europe out
of the Middle East by way of Venice, strove to beautify
their sacred books by means of small engraved blocks impressed cold on damp leather. The books bound for Bishop
Pudsey at Durham in the twelfth century and the Winchester
Domesday Book are fine examples of this early form of
binding decoration. It is interesting to note that a gifted
modern binder, Peter Waters, has revived this eight hundred
years' old method of working blind blocks on damp leather
and some remarkably fine examples of his work are now in
the British Museum, the Victoria and Albert Museum, and
the Broxbourn Library.

Two hundred years later, in the fourteenth century,
Netherland bookbinders introduced the panel stamp, an engraved iron or brass block large enough to cover the entire
side of a small book with blind embossing in one working.
Thus the process of decoration was simplified to meet a
growing demand for books, and the laborious method of
making repeated impressions of small dies fell into disuse.
Another two hundred years passed when again large engraved blocks were brought into use, this time in Lyons in
the sixteenth century for the purpose of covering the sides of
books with gilded patterns in imitation of the elaborate
gold tooling of the period, since such hand work was al-
together too slow and costly a process for the needs of an
expanding book trade.

The first use of gold leaf on the covers of European books
is believed to date from the end of the fifteenth century,
probably at the press of Aldus Manutius in Venice, and the
names of the two great book collectors, Grolier and Maioli,
are associated with the development of the art of building up
elaborate patterns of gold tooling by means of lines, curves,
and small tools. The geometrical patterns of interlaced

straight lines and semicircles, sometimes having the strapwork enriched with painted colour or black, made the
Grolier designs one of the most famous styles of binding.
The Maioli bindings have a somewhat similar character but
the straight lines of Grolier are replaced with flowing scroll-
work and graceful interlacing curves, giving a florid
Italianate elegance to the design.

In the sixteenth century France became the centre of fine
binding, and gold tooling reached its highest perfection of
design and execution in the 'fanfare' bindings with which
the names of Nicholas and Clovis Eve are associated. The
'fanfare' style of ornamentation has an elaborate pattern of
interlaced strapwork bent into circles and ovals, suggestive
of the Maioli designs, the spaces between being filled with
delicate coils, sprays of laurel, bay, and other leafy devices
and a profusion of small decorative tools. Another beautiful
style of decoration believed to have originated with Clovis
Eve is composed of vertical rows of small ovals, each enclosing a flower ornament, and having tiny leaves set about
the line of the ovals, the whole design enclosed in a rich
frame of fillets and sprays of palm and laurel.

Early in the seventeenth century there appeared a new and
magnificent form of 'fanfare' decoration, thought by some
to represent the supreme achievement in French binding,
and generally ascribed to the mysterious 'le Gascon', whose
real name may have been Florimond Badier. These bindings
have the usual 'fanfare' pattern of interlacing strapwork enclosing geometrical compartments but the background is
filled in with a delicate tracery of fine tools, the lines and
curves of which are all formed of dots, known as 'pointillé'
work.

England was slow to abandon the blind panel stamps, and
even the early use of gold was by means of these stamps
nearly one hundred years after gold tooling first made its
appearance in Italy. Much of the early gold tooling in

England followed foreign designs, and the great Collector, Thomas Wotton (1521–87), came to be known as the English Grolier through his use of that style of decoration on his books. During the seventeenth century, Samuel Mearne introduced a new and distinctively English type of decoration known as the 'Cottage' style because of the arrangement of sloping lines at the top and bottom of the centre panel which gave it a resemblance to a cottage roof with wide eaves. The background of the design was filled in with elaborate tooling of sprays of foliage, small rings, scale-like patterns, and numerous small tools, all combining to produce a very sumptuous appearance.

Two other English bookbinders produced distinctive styles of ornamentation, Roger Payne (1739–97) and Cobden-Sanderson (1840–1922). After the massive elaborations of Mearne's Cottage binding, the work of Roger Payne has a striking simplicity, often consisting of no more than a broad framework of great elegance, built up of repeated impressions of small tools said to have been designed and engraved by the binder himself. He usually filled the panels of the spine with decoration worked from the tools used in the side design, so making the back the most elaborate part of the binding, and he endeavoured to make his ornaments appropriate to the subject of the book.

Cobden-Sanderson is the great original among English bookbinders. He belonged to the world of William Morris and the Pre-Raphaelites. The geometrical interlacings and conventional tools of traditional book design had no influence on him: instead he took inspiration from the common flowers and forms of nature, and created from them simple ornaments wherein a natural beauty was enhanced by a delicate and sensitive art. In describing his methods he said, 'I have a separate tool for every separate flower, stalk, bud, leaf, thorn, dot, star, and so on, and I build up my pattern and the motives of them, bit by bit, each composite portion of the pattern or motive, being like the whole pattern, the subject of deliberate arrangement.' His Golden Rule for cover decoration was, 'Beauty is the aim of decoration and not illustration or the expression of ideas,' and beauty of a high order he gave to all the books he bound.

Today the leaders of fashion in bookbinding again reside in France. Their styles of decoration are far removed from the quiet floral beauties of Cobden-Sanderson: they favour patterns of massed lines, flowing lines, radiating lines, lines combed out like the spume of a storm-torn sea. Never has the dexterity of the finisher been so extended as in producing these dazzling patterns of gleaming gold on polished morocco and calf, some with inlays so complex that the original leather of the cover is hard to distinguish. The results are so bizarre, so strikingly modern that students everywhere are hypnotized into imitating, to the best of their abilities, the brilliant displays of these new masters.

## Pasting Down Endpapers

When at last all the tribulations and labours of decorating the cover have been surmounted, more or less triumphantly, one thing only remains to be done before the binding is completed—the endpapers have to be pasted down.

There are two ways of doing this simple job, pasting down 'closed' and pasting down 'open'. A cloth-covered book can be closed and put in the press to set and dry almost as soon as the endpapers are pasted down; the cover is closed on to the pasted paper, the book manipulated slightly to adjust the squares evenly all round, and then left in the press with a reasonable certainty that the endpapers will stick flat to the board and tight to the joints.

This method is unsuitable for a leather-bound book.

Leather being thick material is unable to form as close a fold as is made by cloth when the cover is turned back in an open position so the board, to that extent, is slightly lifted above the joint. This lifting of the board, small as it is, puts a strain on the pasted endpaper when the cover is opened, or may

Thick Fold of Leather

Thin Fold of Cloth

cause creasing along the joint when it is closed. For this reason leather books are pasted down 'open', which means that instead of closing the board on to the pasted paper, as is done with a cloth book, the pasted paper is brought up over the board, smoothed down, and left to dry in the open position.

The slight lifting of the board at the joint also affects the fore-edge of the endpapers, causing them to draw short and so show a wider square on that edge than at the head and tail. This inequality can only be righted by trimming the paste-down leaf to provide the same margins on all three edges. For this reason leather books almost always display a frame of the turn-in leather around the endpaper, and it has become customary to make a feature of this necessity by enlarging it, and decorating it with a blind, or gold, fillet, and so turn it into a pleasing adornment.

The procedure for pasting down 'open' is to lay the book flat with the cover board opened back resting on a small pile of strawboard, or other suitable support, that will fit close into the curve of the spine. The waste protection sheet is carefully removed and any glue, or waste matter, cleaned from the joints. Then the paste-down leaf is drawn tight and even over the board and creased along the joint, and, while held in that position, the line to which it is to be cut is marked with dividers previously set to the required width. These marks must be pierced through the paper so as to show clearly where the cuts are to be made, when the endpaper is turned back again on to a cutting tin laid over the book. When making the head and tail cuts a small tongue of paper, about $\frac{3}{16}''$ long, is left, to be pasted and tucked in behind the joint as a final operation. Both endpapers must be cut with identical margins before starting to paste down.

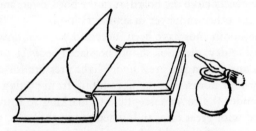

End-paper trimmed out for pasting down.

The endpaper, with a wide waste sheet beneath to protect the book, is now well pasted with thickish paste, and paste rubbed in all along the joint. Then the paste-down leaf is brought over close and even on to the board, nicely adjusted to give equal margins all round, and well smoothed down while covered by a sheet of paper to prevent marking. Some care is required to ensure the endpaper is sticking securely to the edge of the board and in the joint. The board must not be closed until the paste is dry.

Having pasted down one endpaper, the expert will at once turn the book over, without closing the pasted side, and repeat the process with the other endpaper, after which he will stand the book upright with both boards extended, and held apart by a piece of strawboard in which are cut two slots to fit over the boards, and thus exposed to the air, the book is left to dry.

The beginner, however, can simplify the business and avoid risk of accident by dealing with one side at a time, leaving it to dry undisturbed, with the pasted side resting on its pile of strawboards just as it was when the work was completed. Once, or perhaps twice, during this drying period, he will again cover the pasted endpaper with a piece of paper and smooth it all along the joint to make quite sure it is holding firm. Only when it appears quite dry will he gently close the board, turn the book over, and paste down the other endpaper in similar fashion.

When both ends have been successfully pasted down and allowed to dry, the book should be placed between pressing boards and left in the press under light pressure for at least twenty-four hours. The damp resulting from pasting down may render the cover susceptible to marking so it must be handled with great care, and, when put in the press, should have a sheet of clean blotting-paper laid above and below between the book and the pressing boards. On no account should the press be screwed down hard until the following day, lest the natural grain of the leather be flattened. The book should then be looked through carefully, the cover lightly polished with a soft cloth, or cotton wool, and then put back in the press for at least another day, so that all the glue and paste that has gone into the binding may be set firm and hard.

# Machine Bookbinding

————— ❧❧❧◈❧❧❧ —————

The bookbinding described in the foregoing pages is that which was devised and perfected long ago by the old masters of the art, from them brought down through the centuries by succeeding generations of craftsmen, and now practised in schools and the few workshops where fine binding is still their special trade. It remains the ideal method for binding books in ones and twos —but far too laborious for edition work. So an increasing demand for books obliged the binder to seek ways of simplifying the old processes. Thus came two-on sewing, the sawn-in cords, big blocks instead of repeated impressions of small blocks, and the engraved roll for ornamenting covers. The final breaks with tradition came in 1832 when laced-on boards were abandoned for the simpler, speedier method of making the case separate from the book. This small change in binding procedure is now seen as the starting point of modern commercial bookbinding.

At that time publishers sold their books either in sheets or done up in a temporary covering known as paper boards, the expectation being that the purchaser would arrange for a leather binding to suit his own taste and pocket. The first hint that the publisher's binding might aspire to permanence came when William Pickering, a publisher with advanced ideas, brought out his Diamond Classics in 1821 in a cover made in glazed calico. This was draper's material and easily stained by hot glue, but in the ensuing years the calico slowly developed into bookcloth by means of glue-resisting fillings and a variety of embossings, which gave its surface a more acceptable appearance. The lettering, however, on all these early cloth bindings remained the conventional printed paper label of the period, for hand tooling would have been too expensive: only when the making of separate cases enabled the spine to slide into the narrow space between the platen and bed of an Arming press did it become possible to impress an engraved lettering in gold on that spine. It was this gold lettering that gave to cloth binding the finishing touch and transformed the publisher's cover into something an ever increasing number of book buyers were content to retain on their shelves. Thus, publishers with big orders in uniform style, became the binder's chief customers, and single copies in diverse styles, and thirteens as twelves, ceased to be his trade.

Today that trade produces many millions of hard-covered books annually and every important operation in their binding, from folding the printed sheets to jacketing the bound book ready for dispatch to the bookshop, is machine work.

The binder's work starts when he receives from the publisher his binding instructions and a dummy-size copy. This dummy is made up of the right number of pages of the paper to be used in printing the edition; it is immediately bound by hand in a plain case to show the height, width, and thickness of the finished book; this size copy enables the publisher to prepare his jacket design and the binder to do a sketch of the spine lettering. When the lettering sketch is approved a brass block is engraved from it; then sample cases in various cloths are made and blocked and sent to the publisher for his approval. The binder writes into the chosen case all the details of the book, the number of pages and plates, how the edges are to be treated, the weight of board and the name of the cloth for the case, etc., and this case then becomes his pattern case to be used as his guide in binding the whole edition.

Books come to the binder as flat printed sheets, packed in bales of 500, all knocked-up square to avoid damage to the edges. Each sheet will have printed on its two sides 32 or 16 pages, all imposed in a prearranged way to suit the binder's folding-machine. There are many ways of imposing the printed sheets to suit the various makes of folders, and more than one way of printing each imposition, all of which are illustrated in a publication called *Book Impositions* issued by the Master Binders' Association. For speed and economy, most books are printed, as far as possible, on paper of 64-page size, known as quad sheets. These may be arranged to fold as two 32 pp. sections, or four 16s. Since few books divide exactly into multiples of 64 pages, oddments of 16, 8 or 4 pages are printed separately, often two up, and folded on smaller machines.

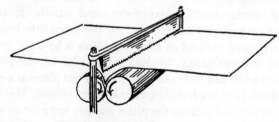

Knife-fold mechanism

Folding-machine mechanism is of two kinds, the knife fold and the buckle. The knife fold was invented in 1851 by William Black, and is still the normal method for modern folders. The sheet is fed into the machine by an automatic feeder, and carried on tapes up to stops which centralize it on the folding table, where a saw-edged knife chops its centre down between the knurled rollers that make the fold: similar knives and rollers below the first, and set parallel, or at right angles to them, make the succeeding folds. Slitters divide the big sheet into sections which then drop into separate troughs. The speed of a folding-machine depends on the nature of the paper, but its output is between eight and ten thousand sections an hour.

In buckle fold machines the sheet travels at speed to stops set between metal plates of half-sheet size. The impact of the paper against the stops causes a buckle to form across the centre of the sheet and this is caught between the rollers and converted into a fold. The folded sheets are placed in a bundling press where, under pressure, they are tied in bundles to await gathering into books.

## Collating

Collating consists of placing plates and maps in the folded sheets, insetting oddments, and cancels, if any, pasting-on endpapers, and gathering the sheets into books.

The normal method of attaching plates is by an $\frac{1}{8}''$ wide edging of paste along the back spine edge of the plate. Modern book designers often prefer to insert plates as 4-pp. wrap rounds, either inside or outside a text section. This is a stronger method because the plates are then sewn in: its disadvantage is that it may make it impossible for the illustration to face the relevant page of the text. Plates when they fall on the outside of section, as well as endpapers, are pasted by machine.

Gathering the sheets into books is now a machine operation. The first gathering machine was invented by J. B. Mercer in 1897 and the modern gatherer follows the general pattern of the original, but has a number of refinements. It consists of a row of boxes each containing a different section of text, a plucking device that extracts the bottom sheet from each box and drops it on to a moving band. When the first sheet has travelled the length of the machine, it carries above it one sheet from each box, and has thus become a

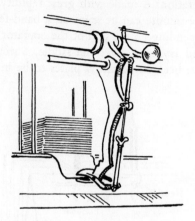

Gathering machine mechanism

complete book. A micrometer adjustment stops the machine and puts out a pointer if the extractor fails to take a sheet from any box. About 25,000 sheets an hour can be gathered on this machine.

## Sewing

The first thread sewing-machine was patented in 1878 by David Smyth, and Smyth machines, greatly changed from that first model, are still in universal use. Stabbers puncture the spine fold of the sheet and then needles, one for each stitch, carry the thread down through the stabbed holes, where a hook catches a loop and draws the thread along to the next hole, through which a second hook lifts it to the surface and holds it there while the needles, again descending, pass through the loop and into the next sheet. The whole series of operations is made with great rapidity and about sixty sheets a minute can be sewn on a hand-fed machine, the speed depending on the skill of the operator in opening the sheet and laying it over the saddle. Sheets in which the bolts have been cut to allow plates to be inserted slow up sewing.

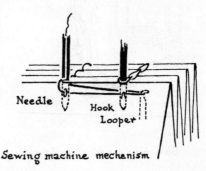

Sewing machine mechanism

In recent years a machine known as the Flexiback Perfect Binder does away with the sewing process for bookbinding. This machine saws off the spine folds of all the sections, reducing the book to a block of single leaves which are immediately reunited by a two-sided edging of polyvinal glue and then covered by a strip of glued fabric, which is crimped to allow for expansion when the book is rounded and jointed.

Nipping is an important process in binding, since books must be uniform in thickness for satisfactory cutting, rounding and backing. There are several makes of nipping presses, but all consist of two powerful jaws, one of which is adjustable and in constant up and down movement. Uniform piles of books are knocked-up square by the operator and placed on a moving belt which carries them into the nipper and out again on the far side.

## Cutting

The first guillotine was invented by Wilson in 1844, but the labour of the plough, and the expectation of an ultimate binding in leather, had established a fashion for uncut edges in publishers' binding which lasted well into the nineteen hundreds. This fashion led to the invention of the Latham Trimmer in 1865 and the Mercer Trimmer in 1900. These machines merely trimmed off the rough extremities from fore-edge and tail and left the bolts to be opened by the paper-knife of the reader.

Modern guillotines are three-knife machines, the fore-edge, as well as the head and tail, being cut in one combined operation. Piles of books are fed into the machine on one side and delivered cut at the other, so that the cutting knives are in continuous motion, and the books pass through in an unbroken stream. As all three cuts are made simultaneously the squareness of the book is assured.

## Gluing Up

The all-important first gluing of the spine is now done by the Jackson Gluer (1929), a simple little machine consisting of a rubber roller revolving in a tank of hot glue, and a scrubbing-brush. Adjustable caterpillar tracks grip the sides of the books and carry them, spine down, first over the glue roller and then across the brush which rubs the glue between the sections.

## Rounding and Backing

The Smyth Rounder and Backer, which came to this country about 1958, performs these two operations at a speed of about 1,500 books an hour. The books are stacked in a hopper and are automatically fed, fore-edge down and one at a time, into the machine, where a former pushes it up between opposed rollers which drag down the outer sections to complete the round: the book is then gripped between jaws shaped like backing boards, while the wiper, with a series of rapid oscillations, forms the joints.

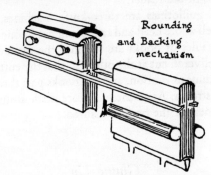

Rounding
and Backing
mechanism

The first backing machine was patented in 1850 by Charles Starr of New York. The books had to be rounded and the joints first hammered over by hand, but the instant grip of the iron jaws of this machine and the adjustable roller with which the shaping of the spine was completed were great improvements on the old backing boards and lying press. In 1903 the Crawley machine arrived from America; it was the first to combine the two processes of rounding and backing; at a speed of 500 books an hour it is still used for books of a size unsuited to the Smyth Backer.

## Smyth Triple Liner

The backed books are lined with mull and crêpe brown paper. When the work was done by hand the books were first stacked, with spines together for gluing, and then re-stacked, fore-edge and spine alternating, for the mull to be attached: the same procedure had to be followed in lining with crêpe paper. All this handling was necessary to avoid the glued spines sticking together. The Smyth Triple Liner cuts out all this hand work. As the name implies, the machine is designed to give the spine three linings, two mulls and one crêpe paper (though in practice the second mull is omitted, if it is likely to cause loose joints): in addition it has a device for gluing on tapes, as well as head and tail bands, when required. Mull, paper and head bands unwind from rolls and are cut and placed in position automatically. An endless chain of clamps carry the books, spine down, through the machine, halting momentarily at each station, the affixing of each lining being preceded by a gluing by a glue roller, and followed by wet pneumatic roller to rub it down. The machine is able to line about 1,000 books an hour.

While the books are being forwarded in the way just described, other machines are cutting boards and cloth to the required size, making them into cases, and blocking the lettering thereon, so that books and cases are both ready at the same time for the final operation of pasting down and pressing.

The boards used in commercial binding are Dutch strawboard, English pulp board, and millboard for special books and certain overseas orders. The sizes in general use are 32″ × 36″ and 28″ × 35″; the weights normally employed are

20 oz. for crown 8vo, for demy 8vo 28 oz., and for larger sizes 2 lb. The first board chopper was designed by Warren de la Rue in 1850, and this type of machine is still used in small binderies. The modern board cutter is a high-speed machine using rotary knives.

Bookcloth is usually 36″ to 38″ wide and made in rolls of 36 yards; for long runs, and to avoid joins in machine case-making, cloth is also bought in quad rolls of 144 yards. There are many kinds of cloth—buckram, cambric, art vellum and canvas, etc., and each variety is made in many colours. Today rising costs of production have encouraged the use of cloth substitutes such as Linson, Glendura, Duralin, etc., strong manilla papers with a finish resembling cloth but costing very much less.

The Smyth Case-making Machine was invented in America in 1890: it did not finally oust hand case-making in this country until after the First World War. It produces about 1,800 cases an hour, with an even gluing and uniformity of size beyond the capability of the hand worker. The Smyth machine uses cloth cut and cornered to the correct case size; an automatic feed places the cloth on a drum which, rotating, carries it across a glue roller; grippers then carry the glued cloth on to a table adjusted to exact case size, leaving the turn-in margins protruding: arms fitted with suction ends lift boards and hollow from hoppers and place them in position on the glued cloth: the table then descends while steel bars push the cloth margins up and inward to form turn-ins at head and tail; a second descent, and other inward moving bars then make the fore-edge turn-ins, after which the finished case passes through a pressing device and drops into a trough.

The Sheridan Case Maker is a much larger machine designed for mass production work. Cloth from a roll slit to case size, passes over a glue roller and thence down the length of the machine, carrying on its glued surface several cases in progressive stages of completion, each case being chopped free at the final turn-in station. It makes about 2,000 cases an hour.

## Blocking

As has been mentioned earlier, the use of the first blocking press, then known as an Arming Press, involved profound changes in binding methods. The Arming Press was first used in 1832. One of the earliest power-driven blocking presses was that invented by John Gough in 1867, the novel feature of which was a cam-operated platen. Modern blocking presses, such as the Chandler Price, have an automatic feed, thermostatic controlled heat, and are designed for both gold and ink working. The output of such a machine is about 2,000 cases an hour.

Today real and imitation gold, silver and all the colour foils are no longer made in leaf form requiring glair wash for blocking purposes; instead the metal and the pigment are ground to powder, sprayed on to cellophane and covered with a dry adhesive that melts at the touch of a hot block. This is manufactured in 200-ft. rolls 20″ wide, the rolls can be slit to any required width, and work in the blocking press as a ribbon unwinding between the heated blocks and the case.

Ribbon blocking has many advantages. It not only does away with washing, and the laying on of gold, etc. but after the impression has been made, the ribbon carries away and coils up all waste material. It also simplifies two-colour workings by the simultaneous blocking of parallel ribbons of different colour.

## Smyth Casing-in Machine

This American invention was patented in 1902 but was not in general use in this country until the nineteen-twenties. The latest model is hopper fed and has a heated former for the automatic rounding of the spine of the case. Rollers coat the endpapers, mull and tapes with paste as the book is carried up through the machine to meet the case. Gripper

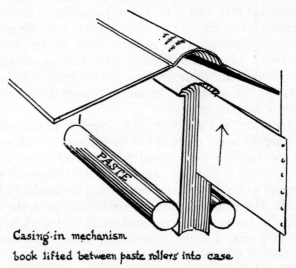

Casing-in mechanism
book lifted between paste rollers into case

arms clasp the cased book along the joints and lift it out on to a delivery slide. The machine works at a speed of about thirty books a minute. The books are then stacked between pressing boards and left in containers to dry. Containers consist of two steel plates, one placed above and the other below the stack of books; these are linked by screw-topped rods at either side. The container full of books is compressed in a pneumatic press where the screw rods are tightened to retain the pressure, after which they are wheeled away and left to dry.

Two important Smyth inventions have recently been introduced into the binding trade, the pressing unit and the jacketing machine. The function of the pressing unit is to do away with the stacking of books between pressing boards in containers, or the old-fashioned standing press, and the hours of delay while they remain there drying. The pressing unit takes the book as it comes from the casing-in machine, and subjects it to a succession of six or eight sharp nips between steel plates that are fitted with heated flanges along their top edges. These hot flanges press deep into the joints, forcing down the cloth of the cover to form a French joint in which the heat starts a rapid evaporation of the damp of the casing-in paste. Thirty-five books pass through the machine each minute, after which they are deemed sufficiently set to be jacketed and packed. The jacketing machine has some resemblance to the Smyth Case-making Machine. Books are fed into a central channel where suction bars lift open the cover boards, other suction devices place the jacket over the open book with flaps protruding, when a bar moves down on either fore-edge, bending the flaps and tucking them under the cover. The operation is all very slick and rapid, and the jackets are positioned with a controlled nicety.

Most of the older machinery in the binding trade was made on the 'in-and-back-again' pattern; the operator laid the book up to the gauge, waited while the machine did its work and then lifted it out again. The latest machines all have a different layout; they are designed for the book to enter at one end and leave at the other, having halted in between for the operation to be completed. Thus a stream of books is able to flow through the machine, unhindered by any return motions, and a greater output is achieved. The grand object of this changed design is, however, to make it possible for several machines to be linked together and so enable a number of separate processes to be transformed into one combined operation, without any halts or handling intervening. Already the engineers have made considerable progress towards the realization of this ambition. With the help of linking conveyor belts, and turning devices, a stream of books is now able to flow through the rounder and backer in a fore-edge down position, turning fore-edge-up to pass through the Triple Liner, and then, again fore-edge-down, to enter the casing-in machine, and so on into the pressing unit—where the jacketing machine stands waiting to give the finishing touch to the production line as soon as a few minor obstacles have been surmounted. Thus a cut book can now be rounded and jointed, lined with mull and crêpe paper, pasted into its case and pressed—and, perhaps, jacketed also—without any handling or break in the chain of operations.

It will be apparent to any hand binder that all this unification of processes not only cuts out the labour of stacking and transporting books between the various operations, but it also deprives the book of those waiting periods which hitherto were considered essential for glue and paste to set and dry undisturbed. Since the results of these new, accelerated methods appear to be quite satisfactory for commercial bookbinding it seems evident that those intermediate halts for drying lost their importance once the disruptive effects of handling and stacking were removed.

It is in the nature of the hand binder to look to the past for guidance, to ponder at every stage of his work, the methods employed by the old masters of the craft in producing bindings that were to survive the centuries. Such considerations are largely irrelevant to the engineer, contriving machines in which rollers, cams, grippers, and the like, can be made to bind books in an acceptable fashion at ten times the speed of the hand worker. However complicated and ingenious the machinery, its way of doing the work is inevitably simple. The hand binder, in order to give the spine a satisfactory round, has to make some half-dozen manipulations and hammerings; the machine achieves an identical result, with a single upward thrust of a shaped former pushing the book between opposed rollers. Such simplified methods are now to be seen in all machine processes; they belong to the new binding of the engineers; their mode of action is as remote from traditional ways as the combine-harvester from the man with the scythe: yet their product is functionally sound and suited to its purpose.

This striving after simpler methods, short cuts, and the elimination of hand work is all part of an unremitting drive for speedier production. As the binder sees it, the book trade is rivalled only by the newspaper industry in its enslavement to the clock; the rush of advance copies, review copies, and publication days, proceeds, in and out of season. The progress of a book from author to reader may begin in midnight calm, but thereafter galley proofs, revisions, and page proofs, have a mysterious way of consuming the weeks and months so that the final stages of passing for press and machining are reached in a fever of urgency, and the printed sheets arrive at last at the binders to a chorus of telephones, echoing the Red Queen's to Alice of 'Faster, Faster', for, however swiftly the machines may run, they still lag behind the expectations of publisher and author.

Of course each new binding development is assailed with the age-old question, 'Will it last?' as if books in all other respects were by nature endowed with immortality. Yet among the multitude of annually published books, how few are remembered beyond their first year of existence; how many clutter the bookshelves in unwanted longevity! Surely a realistic assessment would give a commercially bound book no greater expectation of life than to a shirt or a suit of clothes. A reasonable amount of disintegration would greatly ease the task of clearing out the unwanted. And if those volumes of proved worth, the gilt-edged securities of literature, as it were—if they also arrive at a state requiring the attention of a binder, then the amateur may carry them off to his little workroom, close the door, arrange the familiar tools around him within easy reach, set the glue pot on the stove, and slowly, lovingly, rebind them in strict accord with the ancient rules of the craft. As was said at the beginning of this book, excellent practice is to be gained from such work.

# CHRONOLOGY of BINDING MACHINERY

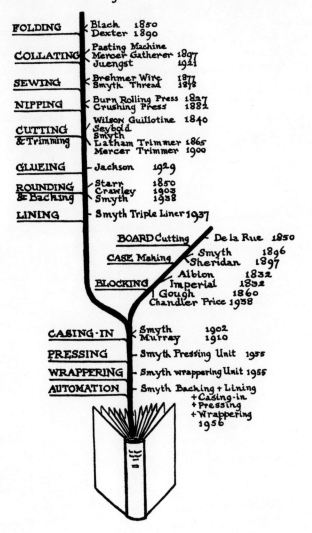

FOLDING — Black 1850
Dexter 1890

COLLATING — Pasting Machine
Mercer Gatherer 1897
Juengst 1921

SEWING — Brehmer Wire 1877
Smyth Thread 1878

NIPPING — Burn Rolling Press 1827
Crushing Press 1882

CUTTING & Trimming — Wilson Guillotine 1840
Seybold
Smyth
Latham Trimmer 1865
Mercer Trimmer 1900

GLUEING — Jackson 1929

ROUNDING & Backing — Starr 1850
Crawley 1903
Smyth 1938

LINING — Smyth Triple Liner 1937

BOARD Cutting — De la Rue 1850

CASE Making — Smyth 1896
Sheridan 1897

BLOCKING — Albion 1832
Imperial 1832
Gough 1860
Chandler Price 1938

CASING-IN — Smyth 1902
Murray 1910

PRESSING — Smyth Pressing Unit 1955

WRAPPERING — Smyth wrappering Unit 1955

AUTOMATION — Smyth Backing + Lining
+ Casing-in
+ Pressing
+ Wrappering
1956

# *Glossary*

———⊶⟨◈⟩⊷———

ARMING PRESS: Early blocking press with a heater-box in the platen used for impressing arms on side of a book.

AZURED TOOLS: Tools on the surface of which close parallel lines are cut.

BACK: The spine of a book.

BACKING BOARDS: Wedge-shaped boards used in jointing the spine.

BANDS: Ridges on the spine caused by the sewing cords.

BAND NIPPERS: Pincers used for nipping up the leather around raised bands.

BLIND: Impressions made with tools on damped leather but without gold.

BLEED: Edges in which the print has been cut into.

BOLTS: Folds which have to be cut before the pages can be read.

BURNISHER: A blood-stone fixed in a handle used for burnishing gilt edges.

CANCELS: Pages containing errors and the corrected pages which replace them.

CUTTING PRESS: A lying press grooved to take the plough.

COLLATING: Checking the sections to ensure they are in right order.

DECKLE: Rough natural edge of hand-made paper.

DOUBLURE: The inner surface of cover when lined with leather and decorated.

DOUBLE CROWN: Paper size 20″ × 30″.

ENDPAPERS: Folded leaves added by the binder at front and back of a book.

EXTRA BINDING: A trade term signifying best work.

FILLET: A straight line on the side of a cover made with a rotating tool of that name.

FINISHING: The lettering and decorating of a book.

FOLDER: A flat bone instrument used for folding paper, etc.

FORE-EDGE: The front edge of a book.

FOREL: Parchment dressed to look like vellum.

FORMAT: The size and shape of a book.

FRENCH GROOVES: A deep concave joint between spine and board.

FORWARDING: A trade term for all operations before decorating the cover.

GATHERING: Assembling the sheets of a book in the right order.

GAUFFERING: Gilt edges decorated with finishing tools.

GILDING: The process of gilding the edges.

GLAIR: The preparation used in gold tooling, made from white of egg or powdered albumen.

GUARDS: Folded strips of paper sewn or pasted into the back of a book.

GUTTER: The spine margin of a page.

HALF-BOUND: When the spine and sides of a cover differ in colour or material.

HEADBAND: Ornamental beading worked in silk thread at head and tail.

HEAD-CAP: Leather at top and tail of spine drawn out to cover the headband.

HOLLOW: The spine of a cased book.

JOINTS: The shoulders of the spine against which the boards hinge.

KETTLE-STITCH: The chain stitch of the sewing linking the sections at head and tail.

LACING-IN: Attaching the boards to the book by the sewing-cords.

MARBLING: The process of colouring paper or edges to imitate marble.

MITRING: Setting the corner turn-ins or joins of a border at an angle of 45°.

MOROCCO: Goatskin leather originating in the country of that name.

MULL: Thin woven fabric used to line the spine.

OVERCASTING: A looping stitch along the back edge made to unite single leaves into sections.

PALLET: A hand tool for making short straight lines.

PANEL STAMPS: Engraved blocks impressed on a cover by means of a press.

PLATE: An illustration printed on different paper from the text.

PLOUGH: The first instrument designed for cutting the edges of a book.

REGISTER: A ribbon marker. The exact alignment of print in folding.

ROLL: A brass wheel with a repeating pattern engraved on its rim.

SAWN-IN: When sewing cords are sunk in saw cuts across the spine.

SEMIS: A repeating pattern made with small tools.

SLIPS: The ends of sewing-cords used for lacing on the boards.

SQUARES: The board margins that protrude beyond the book's edges.

TRIMMING: Edges in which the bolts are left uncut.

TRINDLE: A thin 'U'-shaped metal tool used in flattening the spine of a backed book when the fore-edge is cut.

TOOLING: The decoration of a cover by hand tools.

TUB: The stand on which the lying press rests.

# Bibliography

COCKERELL, DOUGLAS: (Pitman) *Bookbinding and the Care of Books.*

TOWN, LAWRENCE: (Faber) *Bookbinding by Hand.*

HARRISON, T.: (Pitman) *Bookbinding Craft and Industry.*

COUTTS & STEPHEN: (Libraco) *Library Bookbinding.*

CRANE, W. E.: (Upcott Gill) *Bookbinding for Amateurs.*

HARTHAN, J. P.: (H.M.S.O.) *Bookbindings.*

HORNE, H. P.: (Kegan Paul) *The Binding of Books.*

ARNETT, J. A.: *Bibliopegia.*

PRIDEAUX, S. T.: *Historical Sketch of Bookbinding.*

COCKERELL, SYDNEY: (Sheppard Press) *The Repairing of Books.*

MIDDLETON, B. C.: (Hafner) *History of English Craft Bookbinding.*

JENNETT, SÉAN: (Faber) *The Making of Books.*

WILLIAMSON, HUGH: (Oxford) *Methods of Book Design.*

PLENDERLEITH, H. J.: (British Museum) *The Preservation of Leather Bindings.*

COCKERELL, DOUGLAS: (Oxford) *Some Notes on Bookbinding.*

CARTER, JOHN: (Constable) *Binding Variants.*

SADLEIR, MICHAEL: (Constable) *Evolution of Publishers' Binding Styles.*

McLEAN, RUARI: (Faber) *Victorian Book Design.*

HEWITT-BATES, J. S.: (Dryad) *Bookbinding for Schools.*

MATTHEWS, B.: (Bell) *Bookbindings Old and New.*

*Bookbinding and Printers' Warehouse Works* (H.M.S.O.).

LEIGHTON, DOUGLAS: (Dent) *Modern Bookbinding.*

# Index